Finding the Pieces

A Novel By

Sally Glass

Published By

Vabella Publishing

PO Box 1052

Carrollton, Georgia 30112

ISBN: 978-1-957479-08-8

PRINTED IN THE UNITED STATES OF AMERICA

In Memory

of my late husband

George

He said

"How long will you boil in the fire

I said;

"Until I am pure . . ."

Rumi

Art by Annelle Edgar

Prologue

A friend once told me if you stir up the mud in a mud puddle long enough you'll end up with a murky mess that will eventually turn into a boggy swamp.

-s.g.

Suicide

The old Timrod house stood alone on County Road 316, a rarely traveled road in the small town of Riverton, South Carolina. On this beautiful spring morning, a warm breeze tickled Ella Timrod's cheek. Sitting on her porch, she felt renewed. It was time to plant her vegetable garden, a ritual she continued to enjoy in her twilight years. The garden gave her great satisfaction and some meaning to her tormented life. Ella Timrod was a proud and private woman. Even at her age she had held on to her striking beauty. Over the years, her curves had turned into a solid stateliness and she was fit, except for a few health issues. She worked hard and tried to keep moving. It was how one continued in life. But, sometimes she wanted to lay down and die.

Across the road from the Timrod house, a large live oak stood in front of the dilapidated tobacco barns. The oak tree had been there long before Ella was born in the early 1900's and would probably be there long after she was gone. It was a gathering place for folks back when, but those days were long gone, and the emptiness below the huge tree was just another reminder of her own life, old and lonely.

Ella sipped her coffee and slowly leafed through the newspaper. She found the obituary page, folded the paper and brought it closer to her bifocals.

"Old man Ogle died. Well, I'll be. Hmm . . . extended illness. Maybe too much vodka? I didn't even know he was sick," Ella murmured.

She took a sip of coffee and admired her fine Wedgwood cup as she held it up to the sun. She had saved her money to buy the entire twelve-piece setting many years ago. Ella had other china her mother had left her, inherited from a distant past, but the Wedgwood was special, because she had chosen it for herself.

The sound of a truck approaching caught Ella's attention. She glanced down the road, but the sun blinded her for a moment. Shielding her eyes, she saw it was her brother, Newton, and he had the old Ford pickup humming. It was traveling pretty fast. She noticed he kept veering off the road, driving real crazy and stirring up dust on the shoulder. For a moment, Ella thought Newton was drunk from the night before. He hadn't come home, and she figured he was sleeping it off with one of his girlfriends.

When Ella realized what Newton was actually doing, she dropped her cup, shattering it. She looked down at all the broken pieces mixed in with coffee. *No, not my good Wedgwood cup!*

She looked back at the truck approaching the house. It was heading directly toward the giant live oak in front of the tobacco barns. Ella stood watching in horror as Newton drove straight for the oak tree. He waved and smiled at her, then plowed his truck dead on into the old tree.

Steam hissed from the wreckage, and pieces of the truck fell to the ground. All grew silent as Ella stood in shock, mouth agape, looking at the mangled mess.

It seemed like a lifetime before her senses came to her. Shaking off the shock of the situation and covering her mouth at the sight of Newton's body crumpled up against the shattered windshield, Ella calmly walked down the porch steps, crossed the road and checked for life. It was clear her brother was dead. She backed away slowly with her hands covering her mouth. Realizing she was standing in the middle of the road, she quickly walked back into the front yard. Still somewhat in shock she hurried up the porch steps and into the house.

"What to do? Who to call?" Ella mumbled, pacing back and forth in front of the phone. "I'll call the Sheriff."

Her shaking hand dialed the County Sheriff's Office. Mary Worsham answered. "Mary, this is Ella Timrod, please tell the Sheriff I need him out here at the house right away."

Ella glanced out the window at the mangled mess across the road.

"Miss Ella, what is the problem?"

Ella rolled her eyes. "Mary, please do not call me Miss Ella. It's Ella or Miss Timrod. Let me speak with him."

"Good morning Ella, how can I help you on this fine day."

"Your day may be fine but mine has turned into a nightmare. Sheriff, I believe my brother, Newton, has committed suicide. He drove his truck into a tree right in front of the house, and I saw it."

She put her hand to her forehead. "He's dead.

You'd better get out here fast." Ella shook her head. "And we'll need Gaylord Willard Funeral Home to send the hearse." Tears welled up in her eyes.

Ella hung up the phone, straightened her back, wiped away the tears and dialed her only true friend. Bitty Hemingway had worked as a maid for the Timrod family since Bitty was twelve years old. Bitty came from Sandy Creek, a Negro community nearby.

"Bitty, I need you to come over and help me. We're going to have a funeral, and we'll have to get the house ready."

Bitty was silent on the other end of the phone.

"Hello, Bitty, are you there?" Ella said impatiently.

"Is it Newton?" Bitty questioned knowingly.

"Well, it's not me, Bitty, so you can figure out the rest."

"You don't have to be so damned hateful you old . . ." Bitty bit her tongue. "I'll be right over. Got to find Stanley to drive me."

Ella looked back at the crumbled truck. Newton's arm dangled like a rag doll out the window, trickles of blood dripped from his fingertips. She scowled at the sight.

Ella stepped gingerly to avoid the shattered cup. The coffee had run to the edge of the porch and was dripping into the flower bed. Slowly, she picked up each little sliver of china as if it were a tragic piece of her life.

"I swear, Newton, this is your fault. I'll never be able to replace this Wedgwood cup."

1

Memories

From the Timrod farm, CR 316 traveled in a long straight line in both directions. Heading east, it disappeared into the Soul River swamp, then crossed the Soul River on the Wilson Timrod Bridge. It emerged into vast, barren fields bordered by dilapidated tobacco barns and deserted farmhouses.

The old county road was once busy but now long forgotten when the State built the new four-lane to the coast—bypassing Soul County altogether. It seldom received attention from the county or state maintenance and was littered with potholes and broken pavement. One of the poorest counties in the state, Soul County was run for many years by dirty politicians and small-time backwoods criminals.

The tragedy of the day before left Ella restless and sleepless. She stood at her back door in the dark shadows of early morning, staring out across the flat barren farmland. The freshly turned gray earth slowly reflected the coming light. Ground laid open and readied for planting reached out in delineated rows, then faded into the mist and melted into the dark mire of the Soul River swamp. During the blistering heat of summer, Ella would sit on the porch fanning herself with an old church fan. She'd watch the faraway tree line fade into a hazy abyss as humid air arose from the fields in a wavelike mirage. It seemed like the fields and barns were occupied by busy workers only yesterday.

Years back, Ella had decided to lease the land around the house to a local farmer. She had no other family to rely on except her estranged younger brother. Since Newton held no interest in farming or helping her, leasing the land turned out to be a sensible decision. Ella collected the lease payments, watched the tobacco, corn, and soybeans grow, and remembered too many bad times.

When her daddy ran the farm, he turned it into a colossal tobacco operation, one of the largest in South Carolina. Ella had watched the process repeatedly, seeing the field hands wipe the sweat from their brow in the summer heat. She and Bitty supplied them with lunch and soft drinks. Now, along with the tobacco industry, they were mostly dead.

Ella looked at her wrinkled hands and sighed deeply. The first morning rays of sunlight caught Ella's eye. She felt old and tired, especially after yesterday's calamity. As she stepped out into the morning, the rising sun cast a golden hue over the Soul river swamp. Azaleas burst forth with color, and the blossoms of her dogwoods hovered above them like white sentinels; a visual stimulation she looked forward to every spring. She walked out among her flowers, admiring them with little comments, speaking to them as if they understood her every word. She wandered past the aging barn which sheltered her father's old car and a few other odds and ends from the past. A past still haunting her. Walking to the edge of the freshly plowed field, Ella stopped and looked out to the east as the sun appeared through the far off forest. Turning back toward the house, she began thinking about the upcoming day and all she and Bitty had to do.

She stopped and looked across the road where Newton's truck and debris from the collision had been removed by Johnny Todd Towing. The tree would bear the scars forever. It might even die. But probably not. The old Live Oaks were tough as nails. Thinking about her dead brother and why he committed such a selfish act left Ella with many questions. The night had not been good, she had struggled with horrible thoughts, unable to quiet the voices in her head. She left her bed and wandered around the big house in the dark. Midnight memories echoed down the halls and rooms. A dwelling filled with ghosts lost in time; still as alive with horror as if it were yesterday. She did too much thinking on these ramblings. Her demons still whispered in her ear.

2

The Farm

The farm consisted of old family land and adjoining small farms taken by Ella's late father, Wilson Timrod, a greedy, stingy man who gave no quarter when collecting a debt. He took the debtors' land and turned them into share-croppers. Folks joked when he died. They'd say, "The devil put him under a wash pot so he couldn't get a mortgage on hell."

A rapacious man, Wilson Timrod held tightly to the tobacco empire he had accrued; now left to his two remaining children, Ella, and Newton.

The management of the farm fell to Ella since Newton, for a good reason, had lost interest eons ago. Ella was only ten years old when Newton was born. The father blamed Newton for their mother's death following Newton's difficult birth. From what Ella could surmise, Newton considered the land an unmanageable monster. Deep inside, she knew he loved the land, but the darker side left him with resentment and anger. Newton would often turn his back and walk away from his responsibilities at home. Ella, of course, always stepped up to the plate as if it were her plight in life to take care of every little problem that arose and save the world. Now, she didn't have to worry about hired workers. Leasing the land was far better and brought in a nice check at the end of the season.

Ella wandered back into the house, every nook and cranny held a memory. They were fresh in her mind as if it were yesterday; flashbacks appeared like an old movie playing on the walls. Sounds of the past echoed down the halls. Each room held a basketful of memories, some good but mostly bad. Many were so sinister that she tucked them away in the recesses of her mind.

The door to the main dining room stood open to the dining table with a single place setting of her finest silver and china. Ella mostly dined alone. Newton had seldom taken a meal with her, preferring the solitude of his room.

The great den and hallway led to her father's library and office, a place frozen in time since 1971, the year he died. Up the long staircase to the second floor, were sanitized lifeless bedrooms full of antique furniture. The wood floors creaked with every step. Though no one visited, the rooms stood ready. This house would be Ella's burial chamber, or at least that's what it felt like to her.

Somberly, she reflected on her life and the turmoil she had survived. Dismal secrets she held close to the vest, secrets so soul-crushing she dared not let anyone know. A woman of pride, Ella feared she would be scorned in Riverton if such gossip got around.

She pretended her world had been perfect, but its reality occasionally slapped her in the face. She mostly stuffed it away, floating across the surface of her being like a butterfly, sucking the bitter nectar, reliving every traumatic moment until the pain and depression were too much to bear. Somehow, she would find the strength to claw her way back to her fairytale world to resume her halcyon ways.

Ella realized that in every family, there were secrets buried deep in trunks, closets, and other inconspicuous places. Places where some fool had hidden them or written them down and forgotten them, until one day another fool finds them. Ella feared others knowing her business. She could often hear the sound of Newton's typewriter as he flailed away at all hours of the night. *What kind of madness could he be writing?* What Ella failed to discern was that many already knew of the horrors at the Timrod farm. It didn't matter if Newton wrote down the family secrets because people in Riverton already suspected.

Ella attended a two-year women's college and graduated at the top of the class. She knew nothing about life itself, only the rhythm of the farm— spring, summer, fall, and winter. As far as she was concerned, seasons were the only dates on the calendar. The farm was a necessity and allowed the family to survive. It was burned into her soul as if the devil himself stuck the hot, molten iron against her pure white flesh, marking her for life. She wore the brand proudly but ached from its pain.

Her arthritic fingers fiddled with the gold band that dangled from the chain around her neck. Her mind wandered back to her husband, Jacob, lost decades past tragically. Ella met Jacob when he spent his summer working for the Southern Timber Company in Riverton while studying forestry at Clemson College. Ella's love for him was the last of her precious memories. She remembered Jacob so clearly. Ella adored him, and he worshiped her. They were inseparable and spent as much time together as her father would allow.

Wilson Timrod begrudgingly gave them his

blessing to marry, but only if they lived on the farm, where Jacob would work and learn the family business. However, deep in the darkness of Wilson Timrod's mind, he schemed.

Ella wed her Clemson boy after he graduated. The grand event filled the chapel at First United Methodist Church in the heart of Riverton. One year later, Jacob was dead; mysteriously killed while duck hunting with her father in the deep recesses of the Soul River swamp.

Her father described in an emotionally tearful display how Jacob slipped while climbing into the duck blind, dropping his shotgun, which discharged into his chest. He fell back into the dark water, and with all the clothing he had on, he instantly sank to his death. That's how the story went, and not one living soul in the community would ever dare question Wilson Timrod.

Gossip about the death of Ella's young husband floated through the diners and beauty parlors, but only Wilson Timrod knew the truth, and with him is where it died. Something wasn't right. Ella could feel it in her bones, but she dared not confront her father. She feared him, and the fear strangled her life until sometimes she couldn't breathe. Fear is how Wilson Timrod ruled, and this she would always know.

After Jacob's death, Ella's father insisted for the family honor that she drop her married name and take her maiden name back. The Timrod name made people perk up and listen. He said it could catch her any man of the same social standing, but Ella never married again.

Mary Kay, Ella's older sister, fell ill shortly after Jacob's hunting accident. Ella and Bitty nursed Mary Kay and did their best to make her comfortable. She spent most days in bed, not knowing that her father refused to send her somewhere for medical treatment. Since her grim prognosis left her with no hope, he would not waste the money to send Mary Kay to a hospital. She most likely would die even if she did have the best of doctors.

Ella and Bitty Hemingway spent a lot of time together. Bitty gave Ella the sounding board she lacked within her family or the artificial friends who showed up at her door only to see what was happening at the Timrod farm. Bitty would listen, but more than anything, she gave Ella true friendship. Ella never made friends quickly. She forced herself to attend social gatherings and day dreamed at teas and luncheons. She found the social set self serving and a bit boring.

Bitty knew many of the sordid details of what went on in the massive farmhouse over the years. She also learned to keep her mouth shut. To her, it was a house of horrors. Bitty had also experienced the abuse of Wilson Timrod, but those were times you didn't speak of what went on in a wealthy white man's house. You could wake in the middle of the night to a cross burning in your front yard.

Ella's obsession with the juggernaut of a house had just about driven her crazy. The farmhouse had become a burden. Every day there was something else to repair. Too many bad memories walked the halls and rooms. She shamefully hid the ghosts of her past; at least she thought she had. The old house would have killed Ella years ago if not for Bitty. They had worked together every day except Sundays. During the tobacco harvest, everyone on the farm worked from dawn to dusk. The process went on for days. It had to occur, or the moon and stars would fall from the sky.

She leased the farmland, except a portion down by the Swamp that lay overgrown with weeds. During the freshet it would flood. The barns leaned and weren't safe to walk in. Broken down, old trailers and rusted farm machinery stared at Ella from the lifeless shells. She hated the barns and, on occasion, entertained thoughts of setting them ablaze. They would go quickly. What a spectacle it would be. However, that would draw attention, and she couldn't endure any more gossip.

Now Newton was gone, not a single relative left to care for her in her golden years. What would she do? What would become of the home she had known all these years? Would it go to a stranger at auction?

Years after Mary Kay's death, Newton moved all his clothes and personal belongings to her more oversized upstairs bedroom with its private bath. It had an adjoining sitting room at the back of the house and another entrance accessed by an outside staircase.

As Newton grew older, Ella thought he became strange and eccentric. He only came into the central part of the house for meals, and it was rare for him to sit down with her for dinner. He was years younger, and she thought he seemed to lose what little mind he had left as he aged.

Newton kept himself locked away in his room most of the time, so she had no idea what he was doing. He forbade her to enter his room. Bitty was allowed to collect the linens Newton placed outside his door once a week. Then there were the trips he went on, and for weeks he would disappear. God only knew?

Newton desperately wanted to move away, cut his ties, and run far from his dark hole of an existence, but he was tied to the land and house by some mysterious force. He and the old patriarch hated each other to the point that they hardly spoke. The boy was never the man his brothers were. WWII had taken the other boys on the beaches of Normandy. In Wilson Timrod's mind, Newton's brothers had died as heroes and were the real men in the family. He talked about them constantly but seldom mentioned Newton, who would leave the room when his father started on the subject.

Newton was picked at and made fun of because he was shy, so he kept to himself. Most people thought he could handle the teasing, but it was pure torture deep down in Newton's mind. When he turned eighteen, he tried to sign up with the Marines. After his physical, they sent him home. Something was wrong with his heart, which soon became apparent when he found he couldn't hold his own with the farm labor. He required more rest than the others. The heart issue caused the patriarch to reject him further, finally sending him to State College. After his first semester turned out to be a failure, he was back home, occupying the room at the end of the hall.

Newton was quiet and reserved with electric blue eyes and soot-black hair. He would retreat into his room and to an imaginary world away from his oppressive father and the farm life he lived and hated. His room had become a library, sitting room, bedroom, and, at times, an entertainment center for selected confidants.

Ella knew every nook and cranny of the farm with its old stables and tobacco barns. The buildings loomed over the bare land like silent sentinels. Long gone were the days when workers handpicked tobacco, climbing into the rafters where they would hang the tobacco laden sticks to dry by the oil heated furnaces.

Her father had managed it all before illness put him to bed, leaving the responsibility to Newton, his young son. Ella had to beg her father to give Newton a chance to run the family business. She argued that it would be good for him. Newton was a failure at everything as far as Wilson Timrod was concerned, but he gave him the job anyway.

When the tobacco markets opened, men gathered in small groups to discuss the price while listening to the auctioneers' sing-song chants as they walked up and down the mounds of cured tobacco. During the tobacco market, the streets were bustling. Small groups of men spoke lowly about local politics and the unfortunate. It focused on the Timrods, primarily how Newton handled the Timrod business.

After returning from the market each day, Newton would stand at his father's bedside and give him progress reports. He seethed with hatred for his father. At times he thought seriously about taking his pillow and smothering him. He even tried to get Ella to help him, but she would have no part in murdering their father.

When Wilson Timrod finally died, Newton seemed to live again; at least in his way. He never desired to run the family business and dropped it into Ella's lap. Newton began a life of leisure, taking trips, corresponding with strangers through the mail, and a private telephone line to his bedroom.

Ella had no idea where Newton went or what he did on these trips, but it enraged her that he had stuck her with the farm and the upkeep of the vast, old house. As far as Ella could tell, Newton would let the whole place fall into the bowels of Hell before he would plow another field or grow another tobacco plant.

Newton never had a serious relationship with anyone and didn't show any interest in marriage. Ella wasn't sure, but she knew there had to be something wrong with him. The man wasn't right, and she questioned the possibility that he had mental problems. God only knew, and Ella hoped no one else did. She didn't have time to fret over all his issues and her own.

Newton spent most of his days in a robe, lying around his room recovering from the last night's drinking. With a cup of coffee in one hand and a cigarette in the other, he read books and stared out his window at the empty fields surrounding the house. Around dusk, Newton would drive the old ford pickup to join his friends at the local gin joint. Girls loved Newton, but the girls he loved were pure trash; color played a significant role. He would drink until one of the Negro boys would drive him home.

Some nights, Bitty's daughter, Angel, would drive Newton home and assist him up the backstairs to his room. Ella would watch from her bedroom window, noting that Angel wouldn't leave until early the following day most of the time. Ella wondered what Bitty would do if she knew Angel was laid up with Newton in his bedroom? He was old enough to be her daddy.

Bitty had her troubles as well. Angel was as wild as they come. She had a smart mouth and was ultimately out of control. She was Bitty's youngest, born quite a few years after her other children who were married and had their own families. Angel was deep into the civil rights movement, and Bitty was scared that something terrible would happen to her.

Bitty also suspected something was up between Newton and Angel. At least that was the rumor going around Sandy Creek. She wasn't deaf, nor was she blind. She had seen things for herself. While gathering the linens from Newton's room, she found one of Angel's earrings in his sheets. He was way too old for her, but worse than that, he was a white man. Bitty's biggest fear was that Angel's daddy would find out and beat her silly. Things like that just weren't supposed to happen, not in the rural backwoods of South Carolina.

Angel Hemingway didn't care what her backward mama thought. She was beautiful, intelligent, and not about to settle for a lifestyle she knew would lead nowhere. Angel had threatened more than once to run away. Angel loved hanging out with Newton at the local beer joint and would do as she pleased. Angel and Newton went together well and spent hours talking. He was older and intelligent, and this sparked her interest in him.

The nearest establishment for partaking in spirits was the Barbeque Hut in Sandy Creek. The front portion of the building was a small restaurant. Two long tables draped with red and white checkered plastic tablecloths ran from one end of the room to the other. Metal folding chairs lined both sides. For the most part, field hands, construction workers, and the High Sheriff on occasion, would be found shoveling down a plate of pulled pork barbeque with coleslaw and cornbread. There were two windows, one to order food and the other for pickup. Two big sweet tea pitchers sat at a table. Sodas, and beer, would be in a small Emerson icebox in the corner of the room.

Tiny Whitmore was the cook, and she could put out a fine plate of barbeque. She also made a chicken bog that was considered the best in the county. Tiny appeared to consume a good bit of her cooking.

A single door led to a large room in the back

where all the drinking went on. It was a dark, smoky cave with a low ceiling, a couple of windows that hadn't been cleaned in years, a jukebox, and a makeshift bar. Christmas lights hung from the bottom of the bar and ran along the walls to give the room atmosphere. It was a fire trap, and Bitty worried about Angel dying in the place.

Bowman Whitmore owned the establishment but didn't possess a liquor license. You could do a lot in those days if you paid the right man, especially in Soul County. Bowman was a large man of color, at least six feet or more in height. His black hair was combed straight back and plastered down with Royal Crown hairdressing. He was a likable man, but he wouldn't hesitate to stick a knife in your gut or bust your head with a baseball bat if you crossed him. Most colored folks in Sandy Creek stayed clear of Bowman and would never say anything about his business, or they might find themselves floating face up in the Soul River swamp.

The Barbecue Hut was Newton Timrod's hangout. Every night you could find him sitting at the end of the bar drinking with the local girls. Typically, a white man wouldn't be welcome in Bowman's establishment, but Bowman liked Newton and looked after him. Newton always paid his tab and tipped generously. Bowman liked the cash flow when Newton was drinking. It was clear that Bowman didn't want anyone messing with him. Bowman's reputation was such that few wanted to cross him. Newton didn't feel safe at any good ole boy hangouts, and Bowman's was also convenient.

Here was a place where Newton's introversion took a back seat. Here he was outgoing and had a good sense of humor, two traits he never exhibited at home. The girls loved him. Always giving the girls advice, you'd think he was one of the girls himself if one didn't know better. After a few drinks, Newton's effeminate side would begin to show itself. They would laugh while Bowman kept an eye on him, hoping none of the other men would find him offensive.

Ella was disgusted by her brother's time at the Barbeque Hut and refused to speak of Newton's nightly forays. Bitty found it unacceptable as well. The two women pretended it wasn't a reality except when Angel and Bitty got fussing about it. Ella cared deeply for Bitty and knew how badly it affected her good friend.

One day, Bitty came over to help Ella, and she was in a mood, didn't have much to say, and was curt with Ella. Something was up and was weighing heavily on Bitty's mind. After a while, Bitty told her that she and Angel had argued the night before. When Bitty woke that morning, she found a note from Angel saying she was getting out of Sandy Creek to find a better world. While speaking, Bitty kept on working, never looking up. She pushed the broom around the kitchen with rage and anger. Ella knew Bitty well enough to know she didn't want to discuss it anymore. Angel was never brought up again in their conversation.

3

The Funeral Home

Gaylord Willard Funeral Home was a long-standing institution in Riverton. It started in 1879 as a small mercantile store. It also supplied coffins for the small community and found the coffin business far more lucrative than selling supplies. So, the family decided to split the company, one brother running the mercantile and the other brother, Gaylord's grandfather, managing the casket business as the Gaylord Willard Funeral Home. The companies remained small and family-owned, passed down from one generation to another.

However, of late, the mortuary business wasn't as attractive to some family members. It seemed family members were branching out into other companies, leaving the funeral part to Gaylord, himself, and his two sons, Bobby and Stancil. The clan became a little diluted ever since Sissy Willard lost her senses and ran off with a casket salesman years back, only to return with a child. Although her baby boy didn't resemble the Willard family—not one bit, Gaylord took her back, along with her son, Stancil, and accepted him as his own. Many Riverton folk thought it a Christian thing to do, as gossip spread through town like a wind-driven wildfire in a drought-stricken pine forest.

Among the other employees was Juanita Turnbull, the biggest gossip in Riverton. She did the bookkeeping and occasionally helped with a funeral here and there, but only if they were short of help. She didn't like driving the hearse or standing around a cold, damp cemetery or a hot, humid one while constantly checking her ankles for fire ants. It just wasn't her cup of tea. She was, of course, one of the flame fanners. Gossip was her drug of choice, and she just couldn't help talking about people and their problems.

Old man Gaylord was a smooth talker with the sincerity of a Methodist preacher. He was a big man with a deep voice that could charm the bees off a honey jar. Ella wouldn't have any other mortuary bury Newton. As far as she was concerned, the Willards were the best, and they were the only ones in town for a white burial.

The funeral home sat smack in the middle of the historic district of Riverton, your typical small southern town. Riverton's roots were buried deep in the black water of the Soul River, which ran right through its gut. It was also the county seat with an old courthouse and various businesses.

Parnell Evers Feed and Seed store was the main farming center. The Piggly Wiggly was just down the street with a 5 & 10 Cent store next door. Various small shops; mostly shuttered from a lack of business. Historic homes with wrap-around porches lined Rivers Street, where the elderly sat in rockers as they watched the town dry up. Most businesses had moved closer to the new four-lane highway or had closed up entirely, a sign of the times as Riverton was slowly migrating away from its beginnings.

Ella and Bitty had positioned themselves in the front parlor of the funeral home as they waited for Gaylord Willard. Ella perused all the magazines neatly arranged on the end tables. Quickly bored with the magazines, she stood and walked to each portrait. Her thoughts rolled back to her childhood. Her mother would insist she attend funerals. It was the responsibility of the Timrods to participate in funerals. Ella would put on her fake sad face and hug people she barely knew. It made her feel like an imposter. A display casket with artificial flowers occupied one corner in an adjacent room. Ella walked over to it and peered inside the satin-lined, nickel-colored coffin.

"Bitty, if Newton owns a dark blue suit, I think he would look nice in this nickel-colored casket with the pearl white satin lining. What do you think?"

Bitty sat with her skinny arms wrapped tightly over her pocketbook. Her old, wrinkled hands clinched a white handkerchief. She was uncomfortable in the funeral parlor, and she had an attitude written all over her face. Bitty looked at Ella as if Ella had lost her mind.

"Ella, Newton doesn't give a rat's ass what color you pick. Don't you know this is all about you and how things will look on a funeral day? He's stone dead. He doesn't care one bit." She turned away from Ella and muttered, "This place gives me the creeps."

"I heard what you said, Bitty. I may be old, but my hearing is still good." Ella looked down the long corridor knowing she would occupy one of the viewing rooms one day. Bitty adjusted her dress and straightened her back against the chair.

A voice interrupted the two women.

"I am so sorry for your loss, Ella." Gaylord Willard seemed to float across the room as if some unforeseen force carried him ever so lightly. His suit was perfect and had not a wrinkle. His shoes shined to reflect light, and he smelled of aftershave.

He carried a sort of snobbery in his personality. Ella thought that odd, for not one of his forefathers possessed an uppity mannerism. But, she knew Gaylord was indeed a fine, sincere person. A film of sweat glistened on top of his bald head as he reached his hands out to Ella. She stood and cried on cue, helping herself to more tissues. Gaylord gave her a reassuring hug and held her for a moment. He smiled across Ella's shoulder at Bitty.

"And how are you, Ms. Hemingway?" asked Gaylord.

Bitty mashed her lips together and turned her eyes to the ceiling as she fought back the tears. "Just fine. Better than Ella. She saw it all happen." She threw her hand up toward heaven. "Help him, Jesus."

"Yes, that's what I've heard," Gaylord said with a compassionate look.

Ella pulled away from Gaylord. "People are talking, aren't they? They're talking about my poor brother, who was not right in the head."

"Now, Ella, you know how small towns are. Don't worry about such gossip. Anyway, I just want you to know we have done a wonderful job on his face, and, with your permission, I think we'll be able to have an open casket." Gaylord smiled, revealing his perfect dentures. "Newton was a handsome man. It would be a shame for his friends and relatives not to get one last look."

She thought for a moment. "Well, I guess you're right. My brother was a beautiful man. I will miss him so much."

Bitty couldn't believe what she had just heard coming out of Ella's mouth. All Ella ever did was complain about Newton.

"Come, ladies, let's go upstairs to a meeting room and get the paperwork out of the way. Then you can look at caskets."

The old elevator bumped and jerked until it settled on the second floor. The funeral home was the only business in Riverton to have an elevator, which was a small space but large enough to fit a casket. Willard had remodeled the second floor with new carpet and furnishings. It was clear to Ella the funeral business was profitable. She clutched her bag and tissues while Gaylord went over everything. The obituary had to be written, the time set, and the cemetery plot discussed.

Ella dug through her purse for the deed to the plot and laid it out on the table.

"Mother and Father are here. Sister is over on the other side of Mother. My other brothers are in a grave in France. A stone here indicates when and where they were born, died." She went over the entire family, explaining where every dead soul lay.

"Ella, I know every inch of your family plot and others by heart. It is our cemetery, after all."

"Yes, it may be your cemetery, but I own the burial plot," she returned. "I want every little thing to be right." She thought for a moment. "I guess we can put Newton next to Father. Since they despised each other so much, maybe they can work on their father-son relationship in the afterlife."

It was no secret in Riverton that father and son never got along. People would hear the old man reprimanding Newton at the tobacco sales beforc he fell victim to a stroke. Newton's hatred for his father was written all over his face and was apparent to those around him.

From behind Ella, a soft and respectful voice interrupted her thoughts.

"Excuse me, Ms. Timrod. I'm Bobby Willard. So sorry for your loss."

It was as if a younger version of Gaylord had appeared in the room. Bobby, Gaylord's oldest son, helped his father run the business, and Gaylord's adopted son, Stancil, did the body preparation.

Bobby was a neatly dressed young man of medium build and walked with a straight, steady gate, hands clasped reverently in front of him. His demeanor was stiff and protective.

"If you ladies come with me, I'll show you our casket selection," Bobby said as he gestured down the hallway with an open hand.

Bitty couldn't get over how neat and prissy he appeared. She eyeballed him closer, and she could have sworn he had on makeup. He was neat as a pin and good-looking.

Gaylord spoke up. "When you finish with the ladies, we'll take them back to see Newton."

Bobby opened the door to the casket room and directed them in with a sweeping hand.

"After you, ladies."

They stepped through the door into a long, narrow room. The floors creaked, and the ceiling was low. Smaller rooms adjoined the main room, but those doors were closed.

The smell of flowers filled the air—Bitty thought about how funeral flowers have a distinct smell. Bitty sniffed the air.

"Ugh, mums. I'd know that fragrance anywhere." Ella turned and shushed Bitty.

"Take your time, ladies. The prices are attached to each casket. I'll be in my office next door if you have any questions," said Bobby as he left them alone to decide.

Bitty looked around at all the shiny caskets opened up to expose the satin interiors.

"How are you ever going to make up your mind?"

"You're right, Bitty. I have never in my life . . ." Ella was overwhelmed. "They do have a large selection."

Bitty leaned in to Ella so that no one would hear. "Those two give me the creeps. That boy of his ain't natural," she whispered in Ella's ear. "I feel like I'm going to swoon." Bitty patted her forehead with her handkerchief.

"Hush now. They might hear," Ella reminded her. "Bobby's a nice young man, Bitty. At least he stayed in Riverton, unlike some others." Bitty bit her tongue at Ella's comment.

Bitty had not seen Angel in years. For all she knew, Angel was dead. Bitty's sons had moved to the coast, where jobs were more plentiful with better pay. None of Bitty's children wanted to raise a family in Sandy Creek.

"I'm sorry, Bitty, that wasn't nice of me to

bring up that issue."

Bitty's cold gaze penetrated Ella's heart. What Ella said wasn't called for, and she knew it hurt Bitty.

"Oh, look at this one." Ella quickly turned away from Bitty and put her hands on top of a beautiful, handmade oak casket. She glanced at the price tag. "Oh my, this can't be. Surely a box going in the ground can't be this expensive."

Bitty leaned over and took a look at the price. "Lord, Ella, you ain't thinkin' of payin' that kind of money." Bitty stared at her with disbelief. "I can get Stanley to build you a nice pine box."

"I don't believe so, Bitty. Anyway, it would take him a while," Ella said.

"Oh, no. Stanley could put it together in no time," Bitty replied.

"Really?" Ella said, thinking seriously about Bitty's offer, especially after seeing the prices. "No, Bitty, but I appreciate the offer," Ella added.

The beautiful oak casket with its honey wood grain sparkled to perfection.

"I can't afford this one," said Ella.

Ella thought for a minute, looking back and forth from the beautiful oak casket to the cheaper version.

"It will have to be one of the cheap ones." She patted the beautiful casket.

"I do want him to look good, though. People will talk about the cheap casket, or not enough flowers sent, or he didn't have any friends, except for that bunch from Sandy Creek. I don't care. It will have to be this cheap one. It doesn't look too cheap, does it, Bitty?"

Bitty looked at her as though Ella had forgotten where Bitty lived. "What do you mean by Sandy Creek folks?" Bitty cut her eyes at Ella.

Ella wiped a tear from her cheek. "People from small towns can be cruel. I'm talking about the folks from the bar at the Barbecue Hut."

A soft voice from behind the two women drew their attention.

"Ms. Timrod, have you decided?" asked Bobby with a compassionate sorrowfulness smeared all over his face. He was well-schooled in the art of funeral etiquette. "Sometimes this is the hardest part, choosing the right casket, especially if arrangements were not made in advance by the deceased."

Ella looked at the young man with surprise. "I have never thought of doing that. It would take a lot off your loved ones and make sure you got what you wanted instead of being buried in an ugly coffin."

Ella ran her hand across the smooth wood. "I love this one, but I can't afford $8,000.00. I don't have that kind of money," Ella stated.

In fact, Ella sat perched on a fortune, and everybody in town knew so. She felt defeated and just wanted to sit down in the middle of the floor and cry, but she held herself together, pushed her shoulders back, and remembered she was a Timrod.

"My Daddy didn't make all his money by squandering it on caskets for the dead. He would spin in his grave if I spent this much money on a box that will eventually rot." Ella walked over to a bronze-colored casket and looked at the price. "Maybe this one, but can I call you later today? I might want to do something a little different."

"Of course, that will be fine. We just need to know something by tomorrow morning," said Bobby.

"Thank you, Bobby. Where is Gaylord? We're ready to see Newton now."

Ella's face turned hard, knowing the business at hand would be difficult. She hoped they had worked magic on his face because this would be the deciding factor for an open or closed casket, and Ella wanted an open one. "Come, Bitty, let's go and look at Newton."

Gaylord appeared in the doorway. "Now, Ella, you know this is out of our normal routine to let you view him before he is properly dressed and placed in the casket. Are you sure you two want to do this?"

"Of course we do. Don't we, Bitty?"

Bitty reluctantly nodded in agreement, but fear showed in her eyes.

Both women entered the preparation room and leaned into Gaylord's chubby body. His adopted son, Stancil, stood behind the table where Newton lay covered with a sheet.

"Ladies, are you ready?" asked Stancil.

"Yes, I have to see his face. He has to look like himself," said Ella.

Gaylord motioned for Stancil to pull the sheet back no lower than Newton's shoulders.

"Ella, does he meet with your approval?" asked Gaylord.

She couldn't believe what an excellent job Stancil had done. He had performed a miracle.

"Oh my, he looks like he is sleeping, and you

covered the wounds. How did you do this?" asked Ella. She was amazed at the artful work the young man had done on Newton.

"Thank you, Ms. Timrod. I pride myself on my work. It is an art," said Stancil. He smiled at her as though he had just painted a masterpiece, and it was hanging on the wall of the National Gallery.

"I've seen enough," said Ella. "I need to get home. I have tons of work to do. Bitty, do I need anything else while we're in town?"

Bitty's eyes locked on Newton's face. She was amazed at how good he looked. She had not heard a word Ella had said. She was feeling light-headed, and the next thing she knew, she was lying on a couch in the front parlor, blurry white faces staring at her from far above. A strange smell had zapped her back to consciousness. She could see the sweat sparkling like diamonds on Gaylord's bald head. Juanita Turnbull's thick glasses came in and out of focus. Bobby and Stancil hovered in the background like two little cherubs. She thought she was dead and had gone to heaven.

"Bitty, Bitty, wake up, honey. You fainted." Bitty felt a hand on her head and heard Ella's voice calling.

Bitty blinked her eyes several times and

regained her composure. "You say I passed out?"

"Yes, you passed out right beside Newton. I'm so sorry I made you look at him. I should've known better," Ella said.

"Thank the good Lord. For a minute there, I thought I'd died and gone to Heaven," Bitty sat up and fumbled for her pocketbook. "Let's get out of here before I swoon again."

4

Homecoming

The lemon pound cake Ella baked the day before wasn't perfect, but the filling in the center gave it a thick buttery texture. Ella and Bitty sat at the kitchen table, eating cake and drinking coffee. The morning trip to the funeral home had left them exhausted and hungry.

They sat in silence, trying to read each other's thoughts. Finally, Bitty spoke. "Ella, we need to get into Newton's room and find his dark blue suit. That Willard boy at the   funeral home said to bring everything, including underwear, shoes, and socks. I just find that a little odd. There ain't a soul going to see his feet."

"I remember when Daddy died. Newton handled all that stuff. If they requested a full outfit for Daddy, I didn't know a thing about it. I assumed they dressed him in a shirt, tie, and coat. Why would a dead man need pants, underwear, and shoes?"

"My guess?" Bitty laughed. "If Saint Peter lets him into heaven, they don't want him walking around half-naked."

Ella took a sip of her coffee. "Or, it may be that the road to Hell is rough and hot, and the shoes will make that journey a little easier?"

Bitty laughed and sat back in her chair. "Oh Lord, Ella, you know ol' Newton needs to be best dressed. I know Heaven has got to be full of dressed-up people.

"Well, if Newton makes it through the pearly gates, he'll not see too many from Riverton or Sandy Creek."

Laughter filled the kitchen, a much-needed break from all the stress of the morning. Bitty was the only person in Ella's life who understood her and knew how she grew up on the farm. Ella could be herself with Bitty.

Newton's door was locked tight. Not a single key Ella had would open it. They jiggled the doorknob until they were both worn out.

"Let's try the outside entrance," Bitty suggested. "Maybe he left it unlocked before he left on his suicide mission."

The two old ladies slowly made their way outside and around to the back of the large house. It seemed to take forever. Finally, they stood at the bottom of the stairs, out of breath as they looked up the many steps leading to the back entrance.

"Bitty, I'm not sure I have the energy to climb another set of stairs."

"Me neither. Let's just sit down here for a while until we catch our breath."

A quiet came over the two as they looked out over the freshly plowed fields, a yearly task they had witnessed since becoming friends eons ago.

"Bitty, this place has been nothing but heartache for me. I can't live with it, and I can't live without it. I hope my mean, selfish father is resting in Hell. He did some terrible things in his life. He never once stood up for Newton, or me for that matter. I know he killed my husband. I can't prove it and probably never will, but I knew it the day he stood in the living room, surrounded by his cronies, acting like he was so upset about what had happened."

Bitty put her arms around Ella and hugged her. "That was a long time ago. We can't change what has gone by us. You just have to let it go and get on with your life. I know. Your daddy was a mean man."

Ella took Bitty's hand, squeezed it, and held it against her heart. "He was especially hateful to you, Bitty, and I am sorry." Ella gathered her grit and courage, stood up, and stared up the long staircase. "Come on, let's see if that door is unlocked."

The two carefully climbed the stairs, one slow step at a time. At the top, they found a locked door.

"Damn him, with all his secrets. What am I going to do? I need to get to his clothes. That crazy, old eccentric bastard," Ella yelled out in anger. "Guess I will have to call someone to come over and knock this door down. We don't have the strength to do it ourselves, that's for sure," Ella shook the knob with frustration.

Ella flipped through the yellow pages for a locksmith. She didn't want a stranger in her house, and this was proving to be a real challenge because she didn't trust anyone.

Bitty started cleaning the floors and dusting, picking up newspapers, and putting stuff back in order. The muffled sound of a car door out front drew her attention away from dusting. *It must be someone bringing food or flowers.*

Bitty continued her cleaning, listening to Ella's frustration as she made phone calls for help to unlock the bedroom door. *'Bang, bang, bang.'* Bitty jumped out of her skin, startled. *I hate that damn knocker.*

A strange and peculiar feeling came over Bitty. She walked down the hall toward the front door with deliberate caution, reached for the knob, and stopped. Something wasn't right. She opened it slowly. Peeking through a six-inch crack, Bitty saw a woman and a man dressed fashionably. The man was older with gray hair. The woman, whose back was to the door, spoke to the gentleman and didn't realize Bitty had opened the door and watched them.

"May I help you?" Bitty spoke up through the cracked door.

The woman took a deep breath, slowly turned, and looked Bitty straight in the eyes.

"Hello, Momma."

Bitty froze. With her mouth open but nothing coming out, she realized the beautiful woman standing before her was her daughter, Angel. You'd think that a mother who hadn't seen her only daughter in over ten years would become an emotional wreck, but not Bitty. She threw the door open and immediately started on Angel. "Well, look what the cat dragged in."

Angel stared at her mother with discontent. "I see you haven't changed and still have a smart mouth. I guess I got it honestly, Momma." Angel laughed a little and smiled at the gray-haired man.

"What are you doing here?" Bitty leaned to get a better look at the man standing behind Angel. "Is this one of your white sugar daddies?" Bitty asked, pointing to the man.

"No, Momma, this gentleman is Dr. Langford Wallace, a very close friend of mine and an old friend of Newton." Angel felt a bit embarrassed about her mother's rudeness and glared at her mother with contempt.

"So, he's your pimp, and you his highfalutin whore." Bitty laughed at her witty comment.

"Langford, you'd think a person would mellow with age, but no, sir, not my Momma." Angel kept her composure and erupted in laughter.

"Ms. Hemingway, it is a pleasure to meet you. Your daughter works for me . . ."

"Oh, then she's the cleaning lady," Bitty chimed in before Langford could finish his statement.

"No, Ms. Hemingway, she is a nurse practitioner and works with our cardiologist. To put it precisely, she is a brilliant woman and a wonderful asset to our medical group." Langford said all this with the hope that Bitty would understand that her daughter was living a professional life and had transcended the prison of Soul County.

Bitty just stared at the man and then back at Angel. At a loss for words, she finally found her voice with a touch of emotion. "Why didn't you call me and tell me you were okay? I figured you were a drug addict living on the streets. I even wrote you off as dead. Why did you let me suffer so much?" Bitty's eyes teared up. "I've been mad at you for disappearing the way you did."

"Momma, if I hadn't left this place, there's no telling where I would've ended up. Newton was the only one who saw that I was special. He kept me straight." She sniffed back a tear.

"My friendship with Newton wasn't what you and Ms. Timrod imagined." Angel started to cry. "It's me, Momma, and I have worked hard to get where I am. If it hadn't been for Langford and Newton encouraging me, I just don't know . . ."

Angel reached out for her mother, and they embraced.

"Your daddy is going to be so proud of you. Wait till you see him. His old, nappy head is gray, but he still gets around.

"Come in the house. Ella will be glad to see you and your friend, partner, whatever."

Bitty appeared in the kitchen tearful and excited. "Ella, come and see who's here."

Ella slammed the phone book closed with frustration. "I can't let anybody enter my house to unlock Newton's door. When they see what's in his room, it will be all over Riverton."

Ella's imagination had run amok concerning his bedroom and the hidden secrets that might be there. In truth, she had no idea what was in Newton's room.

Ella cautiously followed Bitty, wondering who in the world had arrived. Most likely some nosy members of the Methodist church, who'd go back to Judy's Cut and Style and gossip about what they saw out at the Timrod farm.

Ella stopped dead in her tracks when she saw a black woman and an unfamiliar white man sitting together on her lovely settee.

"Ella, it's my girl, Angel, and her friend. What did you say your name was again?"

"Dr. Langford Wallace. Nice to make your acquaintance, Ms. Timrod."

He stood and offered his hand. Ella looked at it as if it were the hand of the beggar who sat outside the Piggly Wiggly, snobbery showing in her expression.

Ella passed her gaze to the young woman standing next to Langford.

"Angel, it's you, really you?"

"Yes, Ms. Timrod, in the flesh."

"Lord, child, give me a hug."

Even as a young girl, Angel could always see through Ella. She knew the older woman was damaged inside, her pain well concealed.

Bitty couldn't control her excitement. The harsh words that had passed between them had faded.

"Ella, my Angel has got herself an education. She is a . . ." She looked at Angel for help.

"Yes, Ms. Timrod, I'm a nurse practitioner and work in Dr. Wallace's medical facility in Charleston."

Ella was a bit taken aback by what she was hearing. "Well, wonderful for you, Angel. My Lord, it has been at least ten or twelve years since we last laid eyes on you, and just look at you now. All grown up and educated."

"We've got to go and see your daddy," Bitty chimed in. "He's at home watching TV. He'll be so happy to know you're safe and not walking the streets."

Angel looked at Langford and rolled her eyes. Langford chuckled.

"Ms. Timrod, would you mind if Langford sat with you here while Momma and I go to see Daddy together?" Angel asked.

It was evident Ella was unsure about a stranger hanging around the house. The two of them alone made her uneasy, but she relented due to the situation.

"Of course. I'll make a fresh pot of coffee. Would you like a piece of pound cake with your coffee, Dr. Wallace?"

"Yes, please, sounds wonderful."

Ella was caught off guard by having a stranger in her house. The uncomfortable silence between the two was almost deafening. It was only interrupted by the sounds of Langford enjoying his coffee and pound cake and by the grandfather clock, which ticked and chimed softly in a faraway room.

Ella sat erect in her chair, afraid to speak. Her eyes scanned Langford's face as she tried to read his face. She could tell he came from somewhere well-to-do by his immaculate manners. Most likely, he was from one of the old Charleston families. His gray hair seemed long yet neatly combed back into a ponytail. Ella found this a little odd for a Doctor. He was tall and slim with a prominent bone structure on his face. Brilliant blue eyes sparkled in the light. He could be a bit younger than she was, but Ella couldn't tell. He had a certain charm along with his professionalism. Something about him reminded her of her father, but Dr. Wallace was far more sophisticated.

"Well, Ms. Timrod . . ." he paused. "Oh, that's so formal. May I call you Ella?" Langford asked with a big smile, hoping to get her to relax with him.

"Yes, of course, that will be fine. May I call you Langford, Dr. Wallace?"

"By all means."

Now that the ice queen was letting down her ice curtain, Langford felt he should engage her in conversation about his relationship with Newton. "I am so sorry about Newton. We were very close and have been for many years."

Ella let out a sarcastic laugh. "Well, I hardly knew anything about my brother. The older he got, the further apart we became. He shared nothing about any friendships or otherwise with me. All he did was sit at his typewriter late into the night. He left for weeks and never advised me of his comings or goings. He spent most of his life hanging out at the local gin bar in Sandy Creek. I wasn't even allowed to go in his room." She crossed her arms with a huff, and the more she spoke, the angrier she became. "I can't even get in his room to get a proper suit to bury him in." She slammed her hand down on the tabletop, rattling the cups.

Langford finished his last piece of cake and wiped his mouth.

He smiled and said calmly, "I can help you with that issue, Ella."

Ella looked surprised. "What do you mean? Are you going to kick in his door? I'm not sure a man of your age could handle such a feat."

He reached into his pocket and pulled out a couple of keys on a ring.

Ella gasped with frustration. "So, he gives his room keys to a stranger. But not to his sister? Why have I put up with his antics all these years? I should have kicked him out of the house after

Daddy died." She crossed her arms tightly over her chest and let out a disgruntled snort as she glared at Langford.

Langford was quiet for a moment. He looked her dead in the eye. "Ella, I'm not a stranger. I know more about this family than you probably do. We have a lot to talk about, and I hope you will come to understand your brother and why he lived the way he did over the next few days. It will not be easy, but it will be enlightening."

Ella glared back at Langford. "Okay, then let's get him a decent suit to get buried in."

Langford stood up, folded his napkin, and laid it on the table. "Show me the way, Ella, and we'll do just that."

5

The Key

Ella led Langford through the dining room and up the magnificent curved staircase. Portraits of Timrod's past, brothers dressed in uniforms, a sister long dead, and several older gentlemen hung along the walls. Langford was amazed by the magnitude of the old house. Once he was on the second-floor landing, he could see down into the open foyer. An ancient chandelier hung over the center of the entrance hall. Not a speck of dust could be seen on the fixture as the sun sparkled on the crystals and light danced around the room. On the foyer wall facing the front door hung a large portrait of the old man himself, Wilson Timrod. Positioned in a place of prominence, a reminder of who was in charge at the Timrod farm. *How did I miss this when we entered earlier?*

The house was old and well-cared for. Antique furniture lined the long hall on the second floor, closed bedroom doors to prying eyes. Langford couldn't help but wonder about the horrors behind those doors. Beautiful wool rugs lay on the scarred oak floors. Ella pointed out each room.

"And where is your room, Ella?" Langford asked.

"In the opposite direction at the other end of the hall. I have no comfort sleeping anywhere near Newton," she said bitterly. "Here we are. The private bedroom of my lunatic brother."

Langford fished around in his pocket for the keys.

"I'm curious; what are the other keys for?" Ella asked.

"You'll see." Langford smiled, placed the key in the keyhole, and slowly turned the knob, asking, "Are you ready to see how he lived?"

"Let's cut the drama part and open the door," Ella said.

"After you, Ella."

Langford pushed the door open.

Slowly stepping into the dimly lit room, Ella couldn't see until Langford pulled the large drapes back, allowing the sun to break the darkness. The beautiful drapes puddled on the floor, giving the room a softness or almost feminine effect, definitely not the feel of a man's room. She gasped at the sight before her. Everything was neat and clean. Glorious works of art adorned the walls and shelves filled with books. She ran her hand over them, pulling one out. It was the first edition of *To Kill a Mockingbird*.

"Mostly first edition classics," Langford said, waving his hand over the collection. "He leaned toward Southern writers mostly."

"Oh, dear Jesus, I had no idea."

Newton's closet was full of finely tailored suits with matching shirts and ties. His bed was dressed with a gorgeous comforter and matching pillows. Deep forest green with blood-red sheets. On the bed was a dark suit with a white shirt and a beautiful sky blue tie. A pair of leather shoes with socks sat on the floor—a thick envelope with "Ella" written on the front lay on top of the suit.

Langford picked up the envelope. "Ella, this is a personal letter to you. I'll give you some privacy, but if you need me, I'm here." Langford paused, "Umm, Ella? Did you *know* he was seeing a therapist?"

"A therapist?" Ella looked surprised.

"Yes, my dear. Newton was trying to deal with the horrors of his childhood." Langford said gently. "Your brother was a good man. If not for Newton seeing the spark in a young, beautiful woman who wanted to make something of herself instead of staying where she had no chance of developing her great mind, yes, Angel most likely would be an addict or saddled with children with no one but her mother to help her. Newton arranged for her to live with my wife and me and attend college. Newton saw that Angel was special and wanted her to make a good life for herself. He saw that she continued her education, and lucky for me, she fell in love with nursing."

"Well, I never knew he was such a giving man. I thought he and Angel were up to something very wrong. At least that's the way it appeared. You have to understand this is not Charleston; this is a small town off the beaten path, and people here gossip." Ella was dumbfounded by all she was seeing. She sat on his bed and ran her hand across the beautiful comforter. "Newton had exquisite taste; I have to credit him for that."

Langford sat beside her. He held up the keys.

"The other key goes to a lockbox where he left a manuscript he has worked on for years. It's the story of his life here and other adventures."

Ella gasped and covered her mouth. "What in the world has he written about this family?"

"I don't know, Ella, but not to concern yourself with such matters at the moment." Langford gave her a reassuring smile.

"Newton liked nice things, and he was a gentle person. He was writing about his life, reading, music, and art. Newton enjoyed his hobbies," Langford handed her the envelope.

"Before you open it, I have one more piece of news for you, Ella. There is no easy way to put this. Your brother was a gay man, and he had a life partner."

Ella's eyes widened. "I knew something wasn't right with him."

Langford let out a disapproving sigh to her comment. "Ella, Newton's partner, Brian, died last year. He had a brain tumor, and he went quickly. His death broke Newton's heart."

"Well, that is most unfortunate. I didn't realize any of this. But it does explain Newton's absence from the farm for almost three months. I thought something had happened to him. Then he just shows up one day, walks up his back steps, shuts and locks his door, and stays in his room for days, not even speaking to me," she said in a defensive tone.

Ella pressed the envelope to her chest and thought for a moment. "Did you or Angel know that he would kill himself?"

"No, we certainly didn't." Langford dropped his head. "I was devastated when I got his letter, and it was too late to intervene. Angel and I received our envelopes about the time he drove his truck into the tree. He had it all planned, ensuring we would arrive before you got into his room. He explains why in the letter to you. I'll leave you to read."

Langford stepped toward the door. "If you don't mind, I'd like to walk around outside and look at your beautiful flower garden." Langford smiled at her and turned the knob. He turned back. "If you need me, I'm here for you."

6

The Letter

With the arrival of Langford, Ella felt her control slowly slipping away. Her hands trembled, and anxiety washed over her. She held the envelope close to her chest, afraid to open it for what she may read. Thoughts ran through her mind as she contemplated the possibilities.

To whom has Newton left his part of the farm? Maybe to Langford? He would never be accepted in Riverton. He's far too self-important. Or has he given it to someone else? Maybe even one of his Barbeque Hut friends? Why am I having such selfish thoughts? My brother has committed suicide, and I should be worried about what led him to such an act.

She scanned the room for a comfortable place to sit. A wingback chair in the corner of the room looked like an excellent place to read Newton's letter. She eased down into the chair, took a deep breath, and opened the envelope.

Slowly she pulled the pages out and noticed the expensive stationery. *Impeccable taste*. A sense of fear engulfed her as she looked at the letter.

"Well, let's see what he has to say."

Dearest Ella,

My apologies for exiting this world with such an outstanding performance of suicide by an oak tree and Ford F150. I despised that tree, and the truck needed work, so why spend money on an old pickup? It has served its purpose, and so have I.

By now, Angel and Langford are with you, and I hope you will be kind to them. They have been wonderful friends. I know you battle with letting a stranger get to know you. You need to work on this part of your life. The world is filled with beautiful people. There is so much to learn and see. Ella, you are old, and you need to live the rest of your life in happiness. Don't worry about unimportant and small-minded people who gossip about folks they don't know. With that said, I must say you are so blessed to have Bitty as a good friend and confidante. She loves you and has been with you during the worst of times, which I know all about.

I know living with my quirks has been a struggle. I wasn't much of a communicator when it came to our relationship. So sorry!

I left the Will in Langford's hands, and he has my instructions. I know this makes you angry, but these are my wishes. I know you would have jumped right into the Will if you had it in hand, but you'll be seeing it soon.

Now, my reason for committing suicide. Two months ago, I was diagnosed with ALS, and I can't see myself bedridden. So, while I am of sound mind and able to still control my body, I have decided to end it now and save you and my friends the heartache of watching me wither away. Also, a year ago, I lost the love of my life, Brian. I am sure Langford has told you I was gay. I know you will find that unsettling, but that's the way I rolled. Life isn't worth living anymore with my illness and depression from losing Brian.

The suicide of an eccentric, wealthy oddball is far more spectacular than that of your average Joe. The town of Riverton will most likely implode with gossip, and I'll be there in spirit, enjoying every bit of it.

I know you will go down to Gaylord Willard's and cheaply arrange my funeral. I have asked Langford to take care of my funeral service wishes. I know this will upset you, but please do as I ask out of respect. I would do the same for you. Langford will see that my wishes are carried out for my end-of-life celebration. Again, sorry, Ella, but that's the way it goes.

Enjoy the people I've loved and had a good life with. Open that closed, paranoid mind of yours and live. These fine people will help you do that.

On a serious note, Ella, I know how our father took advantage of you and most likely did the same to other young girls. It's time you dealt with your childhood and the horrible abuse inflicted on you by your psychopathic father. We both know what he was.

Please, take advantage of Langford and Angel's help and friendship. They are here for you. I've written all I know about the evil things our father did. Langford has a key to a safe in my room that holds all the secrets. You need closure to the past before your final day.

Know that I have always loved and admired you.

Goodbye,

Newton

Ella slumped into the chair and dropped the letter to the floor. Her heart started pounding, and she could barely breathe. She took deep breaths and let them out slowly. After a while, the panic seemed to ease.

How did he know? I have never told a soul about what daddy did. Tears welled up in her eyes. Sitting down again, Ella rocked back and forth, trying to get a grip on herself. *Oh, sweet Jesus, what am I going to do? He has shared all of our dirty laundries with a stranger. What was he thinking?*

Ella walked to the window. Down below, she could see Langford admiring her azaleas. He turned and looked up in her direction. Their eyes met, and she felt like she had known him her entire life for a moment. He smiled at her, then walked down the path along with the mass plantings of jonquils. Slowly, he meandered along as Ella watched and wondered how she would handle this situation.

Ella realized she would have a guest for a few days. She wasn't happy. Strangers staying in her house would have everyone talking, and with Angel coming back, Sandy Creek would be buzzing. People would ride by to gawk at the home and see where Newton died. Her mind raced with scenarios.

She tucked the letter back into the envelope. Ella was concerned that she would have to relent to Langford concerning the funeral arrangements.

She seethed with anger. *Now, I have to call Gaylord Willard and tell him it's not up to me what happens with Newton's funeral plans.*

In an instant, Ella went into planning mode for the house and Langford, her unwanted guest. It seemed to relieve her of the worries about her past and who else knew. She didn't do well with people around, and this funeral would most likely put her to bed.

Langford found a rocking chair on the porch and took a seat. Across the road, the oak tree looked as if nothing had rammed into it. Only a tiny bit of bark had broken off. He thought about how strong and majestic the old oak tree appeared. He struggled with the idea of Newton killing himself but understood his situation.

The door opened, and Ella stepped out onto the porch. Holding the envelope, she stood in front of Langford.

"So, you're in charge of his last wishes."

"It appears so," Langford said good-naturedly, trying to win her over on the subject.

Ella sat down next to Langford and turned on her charm, hoping it would persuade him to let her handle some of the arrangements. "Langford, will you please share with me his last wishes?"

"Of course." Langford let out a sigh. "First of all, the gathering will be private, with only immediate family and a few selected friends. He left me the list of folks he invited." Langford held it up for Ella to see. "He mailed the invitations early yesterday morning."

Langford could see Ella twitching all over. "A celebration of life catered by the Barbeque Hut will be held here at the house. He specially expressed no religious service. Did you know Newton was an atheist?"

Ella could only shake her head in disbelief.

Langford continued. "He wants his casket set up in the front room for his friends to see him one last time. He is to be cremated and his ashes dumped into the Soul River. That's it."

Ella felt her life flowing out of her as if someone had slit her throat, and it was pouring all over the porch. She could only stare at Langford and couldn't find the words she wanted to say about what she had just heard. She was in shock.

Langford patted her hand. "Ella, these are Newton's last wishes, not yours. It's only right that we follow his request."

She broke down in tears. "But I had such great plans for the funeral," she sobbed, "the showing at the funeral home and seeing everyone. Our preacher at the Methodist Church is an eloquent speaker. I had the music planned." She continued to cry.

Langford spoke up. "Oh, that was another one of his wishes, the music. He wanted a live band."

Ella immediately stopped her crying as if she had turned off a faucet. "What kind of band?"

"An R&B sort of blues band. I believe they played at the Barbeque Hut sometimes. They're called The Soul Men," he said with a laugh.

Ella stiffened. "Oh, my word, absolutely not. I will not have the Barbeque Hut bunch here on my property."

"Ella, it's too late. The Newton plan is already in motion. He's got it all covered. The obituary is written advising services are private and by invitation only."

The ringing of the phone startled her. "Who could this be?" She hustled inside to answer.

"Ella, this is Gaylord Willard. We need to talk."

"Yes, I know, Gaylord. Plans have changed. I'll get the suit to you today and explain everything." She turned to find Langford listening to her.

"Ella, let's do what's right and respect Newton's wishes."

"I guess I'll have to. I'm sure by now that Bitty is on board. No doubt Angel has told her," Ella sighed curtly. "Well, let's get Newton's clothes and get over to the funeral home."

Ella retrieved her purse and car keys from the kitchen while Langford went up to Newton's room and got the suit.

"Come on, let's go," Ella called up to Langford. "I'm not leaving you here by yourself. I'll not have a stranger snooping around in my house."

Langford rolled his eyes and followed Ella outside. She pulled her old Buick Regal out of the carport. It looked brand new. Langford placed his coat in the back seat and climbed into the passenger side.

"Well, I'm looking forward to seeing Riverton and meeting the funeral director. I have Newton's wishes in my briefcase." He patted it with his hand.

Ella looked at Langford with ambivalence. "Oh well, I guess you have his Will in there?"

Langford smiled. "I do."

She started the car and slowly turned onto County Road 316 toward Riverton.

7

The Reunion

It had been a long, busy, crazy day for Bitty. She couldn't stop talking to Angel about what had transpired that morning at the funeral home and how Ella had witnessed the suicide. Bitty went on about every little thing in Soul County over the years of Angel's absence. She brought Angel up to date about her brothers, nephews, and nieces and how they were doing in school. She filled her in on all the Sandy Creek gossip, Angel's old friends, the ones who were good family girls, married and raising kids, and the ones, as Bitty put it, who were good-for-nothing drug addicts.

Angel already knew all about her family. Her older brother, Maurice, knew where she had gone, and he swore to silence. He had kept her up with any news coming out of Sandy Creek. She knew her other brothers would be hopping mad at her for not staying in touch, but she would deal with that at another time. She had to explain to her father why she had left. She remembered he had a little bit of a temper and hoped that he had mellowed some with age.

Sandy Creek Road meandered along the edge of the Soul River swamp until it ended in the small community of its namesake, Sandy Creek. Angel noticed some new houses, and a couple of businesses had sprung up since she had left.

"I have to make one stop before we go see Daddy." Angel looked at her mother to see if she would mind.

"Where do you want to stop? I want you to see your daddy."

"It will only take a few minutes. Daddy doesn't even know I'm here. It's been over ten years; a few more minutes won't matter."

Angel pulled into the Barbeque Hut, and Bitty hit the ceiling.

"You gotta be joking. Are you going to Bowman's place?"

"Yes, ma'am, we are."

"Oh no, I'm not going in there. Bowman sells alcohol. I'll go to the restaurant side but not that den of sinners hole in the back.

Angel couldn't help but snicker.

"It'll be fine, Momma. I have something important to speak to Bowman about."

"I'll sit right here in the car, and you go on doing what you need to do."

"Okay, I don't want you to do anything that makes you feel uncomfortable. Will you be okay?

"You bet. I know all the criminals around. Don't worry. " Bitty patted her purse and smiled.

Angel knew right off that her mama was armed and ready. "I'll be right back."

Angel walked behind the Barbeque Hut to the bar entrance. Sitting at a table smoking a cigar and drinking a cup of coffee was Bowman Whitmire. He was one of the meanest men in Sandy Creek, but the people who knew Bowman knew he had a good heart toward anyone who spoke the truth.

"Sorry, not open yet. Bar opens at five," he said without looking up from his paper. It was dark and gloomy, with a bit of sunlight peeking through the dirty window allowing him to read.

Angel walked toward him. He looked old and grumpy, hair graying and beard slightly scraggly— his fingernails stained from years of cigar smoking.

"Girl, didn't you hear what I said? We ain't open till five," he said, squinting to look at the woman standing in front of him. "Lord have mercy if it ain't Angel Hemingway." Bowman struggled to stand, grabbed his cane, and pushed upon it. "Well, you are a sight for sore eyes. Give me a hug."

Angel leaned forward and hugged his neck. The smell of smoke and an old man wafted up around him.

"Bowman, how are you? So good to see you," she said with a smile. Tears welled up in her eyes.

She looked around the room. Not much had changed. Bowman had a better selection of whiskeys and beer taps behind the bar. A small stage at the back of the room was new, and a jukebox in the corner. The Christmas tree lights were still hanging. *Indeed he had changed them over the years.*

Her mind flashed back to all the nights she'd hung out with Newton at the end of the bar. They'd spend hours together talking about life beyond Sandy Creek. So many memories.

Angel was too young to be in the place, but Bowman overlooked her age and only served her sodas. As far as she knew, he never sold alcohol to minors.

Bowman eased himself back into his chair and hung his cane over the table's edge.

"Well now, look at you all dressed up and professional-looking. A few tears ran down Bowman's face. He wiped his eyes with a napkin that looked like it had been on the table for days. "Would you like a drink or a cup of coffee?"

"No, thank you. Momma's waiting in the car. I'm here for the funeral."

Bowman shook his head in disbelief. "I can't believe my friend was so deeply depressed. Newton always put on a happy face when he came in. I knew he was sick, but I never mentioned it, and neither did anyone else. Being gay is okay with me. He didn't hurt a soul. He did, over the years, share stuff with me about his mean old daddy, stuff that no sane man or woman would want to hear. I guess I should've known. I witnessed it."

"I know. I was shocked as well. I had no idea. It's called hidden depression. Depressed folks put on one face to friends and family, but are torn apart on the inside."

Angel fought back the tears. *Newton had it planned down to every little detail,* she thought.

"He was a friend to me, too, Bowman. We had so many good times sitting at the end of your bar." She patted Bowman's hand.

"I wanted to check in on you." She paused. "Did you get the letter and invitation?"

Bowman dropped his head. The letter lay open on the table in front of him. He tapped his finger on it. "I did, and I know what I have to do when the time comes."

"Can you do it, Bowman?"

"Yes'um, I can, and I will. I'll do it for Newton. As for the other request, I got Junior getting the food and all. He and his wife took over the restaurant, and they're doing a fine job. Tiny passed over a few years ago. Man, do I miss that woman's cooking. She made the best chicken bog in Soul county. I surely do miss her, but Junior is doing a good job, yes sir, real fine. He's brought in some new recipes and is cooking the meat differently. I leave all that to him just as long as the dollars come in and people are happy."

"What about the band?" Angel asked.

"Yep, got them, too. The boys stay busy playing all over, especially down on the coast, but they'll be here."

Angel let out a sigh of relief.

"Thanks, Bowman. I think Newton's celebration of life is going to be interesting."

"I agree. I've never been to the Timrod house for a party. I've delivered moonshine way back. Didn't much like going around the place."

She stood, and he started to get up.

"No, don't get up. I have to run. Going to see Daddy."

A horrible deep cough grabbed hold of Bowman, and he bent over in a spasm.

"Sorry, I got a touch of emphysema." Bowman wiped his mouth with his napkin.

"You know, your daddy never said much to anyone after you left. He just went silent and did his wood carving. I know he'll be glad to see you. I like your daddy. As for Bitty, that momma of yours, she won't give me the time of day." Bowman laughed a little. "She's okay, though."

He paused a minute. "Angel, when you get old and sick, you look at everything differently."

Angel smiled. "I know; I see it every day in my line of work."

"See you later, baby girl." Bowman went back to reading his paper.

When Angel returned to the car, she found her mother in a mood. She could tell by how she had her lips narrowed, and arms crossed over her chest.

"What's wrong, Momma? You've got the upset look on your face I remember from years ago."

Bitty sat silent. Looking away from Angel, she finally spoke up. "I want to know why you never contacted me all those years. You let us think you were gone forever. We had all sorts of ideas about what happened to you, and they were bad ones."

Angel took a deep breath and slumped in her seat a bit. "I was so mad at you and Daddy. I wanted to run away from Sandy Creek. I was confused and upset no body understood my feelings except Newton."

"Where did you go that night?" Bitty questioned.

Angel gathered her thoughts.

"I packed my clothes or as many as I could get in my small carry case, and I climbed out my window and started walking toward the Barbecue Hut. I knew it would be closed, but maybe Bowman might still be around. I was going to borrow money from him to get a bus ticket to Atlanta.

"Sure enough, he was inside, counting his money and cleaning up. He didn't answer at first. I banged again. He jerked it open with a gun pointed at my head. Scared me to death. Inside, I told him what happened, and he sat me down, gave me a coke, and called Newton. In a bit, Newton arrived, and we all had a long talk.

"Newton had found Langford at that time, and they had become close, close enough for Langford and his wonderful wife to take me in. Newton drove me to Charleston at daybreak, where my new life began. Trust me; it was difficult. I had to catch up on subjects I had fallen behind in school, and Newton was right there to help, as was Langford."

Bitty was curious how she got into school without her parents to sign. "So, you did this school on your own?"

"Momma, I was eighteen, old enough to have my checking account. Newton deposited the money I needed to go to school, and I worked on getting small scholarships through my first and second years. Langford did a little backdoor work to get me into the suitable classes when I decided to get my degree in nursing.

"My classes were challenging. Nursing isn't an easy subject, but I caught on and continued making the grade. When I graduated, I decided to specialize in cardiology. But before doing so, I learned as a floor nurse. I continued my studies, and, upon completion, I went to work at Langford's medical group."

"You still haven't answered my question. Why didn't you call us?"

Angel sighed. "Oh, Momma, I wanted to so many times, but my anger with you and Daddy was still buried deep inside, and until I could work on that part of my life, I felt it best not to call. Finally, I did call Maurice. He came to Charleston. We talked about my decision not to contact you, and he agreed to keep the secret until I was ready to see you. Please, don't be mad at him. I am thankful for all my brothers, especially him. He kept me up to date with both of you."

Bitty was surprised that Maurice hadn't said a word to them. Usually, he was a blabbermouth. Bitty seemed pretty satisfied with all she had heard but was still hurt that Angel hadn't called them.

"Momma, Newton had been after me to get in touch. So had Langford. When I got my letter from Newton," she paused, tears brimming her eyes.

"He said he was relieved that I would finally see you and Daddy."

She wiped her face. Bitty handed her a tissue.

"I'm sorry, Momma, anger got the best of me." She took a deep breath.

"Working as a cardiology nurse, I've learned that life could be short, and making amends is the best way to move on. I love you, Momma. Please forgive me for the pain I caused you."

The women latched onto each other, cried, and hugged until they felt the guilt flow away, and nothing but love for each other was left.

Stanley Hemingway spent his days relaxing in his recliner and watching *The Price is Right* and his favorite soap opera, *The Young and the Restless*. When he felt up to it, he managed to do some woodworking in his workshop, making furniture for folks now and then.

Stanley became a recluse when Angel ran away. He didn't know where she had gone, and since Angel was eighteen at the time, the local police had no interest in finding her. Bitty and Stanley thought she could have been abducted, raped, murdered, and buried deep in the Soul River swamp. That criminal sort, colored and white, did linger in the area. Meanness didn't discriminate.

What worked on Stanley and Bitty was that they had argued the night before Angel ran away. This burden set in on Stanley, and he had carried it with him ever since.

Angel and Bitty pulled up in front of the house. Bitty jumped out first. She put her hands up to stop Angel from going inside. "Now listen, I'm not sure how your daddy will take this, so we need to ease it on him. He's old and has a few heart issues."

"Okay, Momma, how do you want me to handle it?"

"Let me go in first and grease the skids. I don't want your daddy dropping dead on us," Bitty said with concern."

Angel laughed a little and rolled her eyes in the infamous way Bitty remembered from Angel's teenage years.

"I'll wait right here on the porch. Go on in, and let's get this over with."

Angel stood next to the front door and listened. She could only hear mumbling that went up and down in frequency. She stepped away from the door and stood in the front yard, looking at her mother's daylilies popping up out of the ground. A loud noise startled her. She turned as the front door flew open, slamming the screen door against the wall. All she saw was her daddy coming at her with arms wide open. He took her in and squeezed her until she almost lost her breath.

"Oh, dear Jesus, you have brought my baby girl home. I knew in my heart you would come home one day."

Tears poured out of Stanley's eyes. He plopped down on the steps, pulling her down with him. He couldn't stop hugging her. Several nosy neighbors saw the commotion and started wandering into the yard.

Stanley, Angel, and Bitty were in tears, laughing and hugging. Suddenly, three neighbor women broke into song and clapped their hands, singing praises to the Lord.

Laughter could be heard way into the evening long after the sunset over the Soul River swamp. Angel had come home.

8

The Will

I f Hell existed, Ella was in it sitting next to the fallen angel, himself. The last two days had left her life turned upside down. She had everything planned until Langford Wallace and Angel Hemingway showed up. Now she had to relinquish the funeral arrangements to Langford, since Newton had made his wishes clear in his letter.

The meeting at the funeral home was leaving her feeling empty and out of control. Langford explained everything to Gaylord and his sons. They stood around him listening as if he were a mythical god with his Charleston dialect and expensive clothes. He explained that Newton wanted his casket to be taken to the house on Friday afternoon for viewing the next morning. Langford also invited the Willards to the barbeque. They hadn't received a formal invitation, but Langford felt they should be there for all the good work they had put into making Newton presentable.

Gaylord Willard held the suit Newton had picked out along with the shoes and socks. Gaylord leaned into Langford and whispered so Ella wouldn't hear. "We'll put him in the cooler until Friday morning."

Gaylord nodded to his sons as he handed the suit to Bobby.

Ella sat quietly, listening to the conversation. She couldn't believe what she was hearing. She had run the house and the leasing of the land for years, and now a complete stranger had entered her life and taken over.

After a while, she tuned them out. She stared out the window at Clarence Bishop's house across the street from the funeral home, making a mental note on how it had started to look run down. Clarence had been a fine attorney, handling only criminal law, but his wife had caught him with his secretary years back. Ella remembered the sleazy girl he had working for him. When his wife, Sarah Jo, found out from one of her friends that something was going on, she busted into his office and found them going at it right on his desk. It wasn't long before the girl moved out of town. From then on, Clarence walked a straight line.

Ella chuckled to herself as she thought about the underbelly of Riverton. She always found a place to go to in her mind when the stress of life seemed to take a tight grip on her, and right now her thoughts were trying to sort out why Clarence had let such a beautiful old home go into disrepair. His wife passed away two years ago. Ella just figured he didn't care anymore about how his house and yard looked. Ella's concern about the house of an old man, who she probably hadn't spoken to in years, was her comfort place at the moment.

"Ella, does this work for you?" Langford asked.

"What?" She snapped back to the task at hand. "Oh, whatever Newton wanted, that's what he'll get. Seems it's always been that way," she said in a curt tone.

"Now, Ella!" Langford looked at her with a smile on his face.

"Well, it's true. After Daddy died, Newton pretty much did what he wanted."

"Oh well, I'm not having that conversation with you at this time, Ella. Our next stop is Attorney Rivers."

"But it's 4:30, and I'm not sure he'll still be in his office. He usually goes over to the American Legion and drinks. He's a war hero, you know, Purple Heart and all," she said with a bit of snobbery in her voice.

"Really? I guess he deserves a drink or two if he has a Purple Heart." Langford looked impressed. "Let's stop and see, by chance, if he's still in his office."

Leaving the funeral home, Langford escorted Ella to the car, opening the driver's door for her before getting in himself.

A man with manners. Far and few between these days, especially around here. For once, she gave Langford a smile. She turned the ignition over and drove to Rivers Law Firm.

It so happened that Earl Rivers had been in court all day and had just returned to his office. When Langford and Ella walked through the door, he was explaining to his paralegal what had transpired over the day. Turning and seeing Ella, he opened his arms and gave her a hug. "I'm so sorry to hear about Newton, Ella."

He then offered his hand and introduced himself. "Earl Rivers," he grabbed Langford's extended hand with a good hard shake.

"Dr. Langford Wallace."

"Dr. Wallace and Newton were very close friends," Ella forced a fake smile across her face.

"A pleasure to meet you, Dr. Wallace. Welcome

to Riverton."

"Please, call me Langford."

"Sure enough." Bill laid his files down on his assistant's desk. "Is this a business call, Ella?"

"Earl, we need to have Newton's Will probated."

Attorney Rivers looked a little confused. "I didn't realize Newton had a Will. At least I never drew one up for him. Good Lord, I've been doing your legal work for years and a few things for Newton."

Langford spoke up. "It seems he had an attorney in Charleston do the Will. Newton didn't want anyone around Riverton to know about his wishes or business."

Earl motioned down the hallway toward his office. The two men walked shoulder to shoulder talking about unimportant subjects Ella could care less about.

"So, Ella, I guess he made you Executrix?"

"One would assume so, since I am his only surviving family member." She looked at Langford and gave him a sarcastic smile. "He did state in a letter to me that Langford is to see over the funeral arrangements." She gestured with a flip of her hand toward Langford.

Earl put his bifocals on. "Hmm, okay let's see

it." He motioned for them to have a seat.

Langford reached into his briefcase, pulled out the Will and handed it to Attorney Rivers. Earl leaned back in his chair and slowly flipped through the pages.

"Well, Ella, this is what I know you'd like to hear about first. Newton has left the house and most of the land to you." He paused and waited to see what kind of reaction Ella would have.

"That's the way it should be, since I am the only one left. Wait, what do you mean most of the land?"

Earl Rivers laughed a little. "Okay, here's what he has also done." He smiled and leaned forward.

Earl looked over his bifocals at Ella and Langford. "When old man Sumpter couldn't pay his debt, your daddy grabbed up the Sumpter farmland. Newton has given the Sumpter farm back to Jay Sumpter."

Ella almost fell out of her chair. "What? This can't be."

"What an act of kindness," Langford said.

Ella snapped her head around and looked at Langford as if he were a crazy man. "That cuts off almost three hundred acres."

Langford shook his head in disgust. "Ella, with all the land you now own, do you really think a mere three hundred acres will make a difference in the long run?"

Ella was beside herself. "But, Earl, that is some of the prettiest land we owned. It runs all the way to the Soul River swamp.

The attorney sighed. "Ella, this will give Jay Sumpter a chance at something he's always wanted to do, farm his family land.

"Sorry, Ella, unless you want to spend a bunch of money fighting it in court, there's not a thing you can do about it, because the Sumpter farm is part of Newton's inheritance from your father. What's done is done."

Ella stared at Earl Rivers with disgust. "Well, I guess I will have to live with it."

Earl tapped his pen on his desk and continued to study the Will. "Wait a minute now. Here are the specific bequests."

"Oh, good Lord, now what," Ella said impatiently.

"He's leaving his entire book collection to the Soul County Public Library and his art collection to the State Museum in Columbia."

Ella was over the edge now.

Earl laughed. "He's made a good decision with the art. Our state needs more people to leave their art collections for others to enjoy."

Ella shook her head. "Whatever."

"Okay, folks, I'll get the probate process started. This may take about a year."

Earl put the Will back in its folder, then buzzed for his assistant, who immediately appeared at the door.

"Stacy, honey, make copies of this Will for Ms. Timrod and Dr. Wallace, please."

Langford noticed a wall of photographs. One was of a group of soldiers kneeling with arms over shoulders looking young and filled with piss and vinegar. He decided to use them to change the mood in the room. "Great photographs. See you served in Nam."

"Yep, 5th Special Forces Group." He looked at Ella. "Ella, if you and Langford want to join me over at the American Legion, we can have a drink and talk about the old days in Riverton. What do you say?"

"No, Earl. You know I don't go to places where alcohol is served."

Earl laughed, glanced at Langford and winked.

"Okay, Ella, but a stiff drink might do you good."

Earl grabbed his coat and headed to the door. Ella and Langford followed. Outside, Earl shook Langford's hand once more and hugged Ella. "If you need anything, call the office, and Stacy will get the message to me."

Earl smiled, then walked down the street past the courthouse and entered the American Legion.

9

The Bequest

Jay Sumpter was tired and dirty from his long day working at the local car dealership changing oil and rotating tires. This wasn't the life he aspired to, but it was what fate had dealt him. He wanted to be a farmer from the day he could walk and talk. He remembered as a little boy riding on the tractor with his dad when he plowed their three hundred acres next to their house.

Jay was eight years old when his dad lost the land to Wilson Timrod. All the fun died as he watched his dad drink himself to death, unable to forgive himself for something he had no control over, the weather. A drought had taken their entire crop, not only theirs but that of many other farms in Soul County. Jay's father had borrowed money from the bank to plant the crop. When the loan was called he couldn't pay, and old man Timrod jumped right on it. Crooked lawyers and judges whose back pockets were filled with Timrod money ruled against his dad. There was nothing to be done. As Jay grew up, he heard rumors and was sure the old bastard had his hands deep in the bank's pockets, as well.

Every time Jay made the half-mile drive up his road to home, he could see what could have been his. All he had to do was jump the ditch, and he would be standing on his dream, but it wasn't his land, and the posted signs sent that message. The signs were always a reminder of what a greedy man Wilson Timrod was. Jay tried to hide the hatred he had for the Timrods, but after a few beers it came out in tears and fists to the barn wall.

The aged barn behind the farmhouse had a slight lean but stood proudly. A few pieces of dated equipment, and implements were still scattered around. Tractor hoods were left open where Jay had worked on them. On the weekends, he would retreat there with a six-pack and fiddle with the old stuff. His wife, Sonia, and Jay, Jr. would join him, and they'd talk about their dream of living the farm life with some livestock and maybe even a couple of horses. Jay Jr. was a member of the FFA and was learning a new way to farm, if he only had the land to do it on.

Jay and Sonia were strapped for money, even with both of them working. Every penny went into keeping up the old farmhouse. They had dreams, especially for their son. He wanted to go to college and study agriculture. He was a straight A student, and hopefully there would be some scholarship money for him.

Jay stopped at his mailbox, reached in and pulled out a handful of magazines and bills. He threw the bundle on the passenger seat and noticed a handwritten envelope addressed to him and his wife. He picked it out of the bundle, looked it over and saw the return address was the Timrod farm.

"Damn, a letter from a dead man, Newton Timrod, himself." He pulled over, turned off the ignition and opened the letter.

Dear Jay and Sonia,

First of all, I'd like to invite you and your family to a barbeque this Saturday at Ella's house. It will begin around 1:00 p.m. and is by invitation only. Everyone there is a friend of mine. They're from all over. You'll meet some very interesting folks. I hope you will attend, but if you don't, that's fine, too.

Now, the real reason for this letter. I know you and Sonia have struggled through the years trying to hang on to what is left of your family farm. I want you to know that Ella and I had nothing to do with what my father did to your family. Instead of reaching out and trying to help your father, the greed in him saw an opportunity to enhance his own kingdom. My father never stopped wanting more. He was actually confined to his bed when he had his attorney handle the buyout. I ask myself why, at his old age, he continued to steal land out from under our neighbors? I'm sure my father is resting in Hell right now for the meanness in his heart.

Jay, please accept my apologies. As I said, Ella and I had nothing to do with what went on. Also, in my Will, I have gifted the entire 300 acres back to you and your wife. Ella most likely will use Billy Rivers as her attorney, and he will be in touch to explain everything and how it will play out.

Jay, I hope you will prosper and become the farmer you have always wanted to be. One other issue, the taxes on the land will be paid for the next five years to give you a chance to get the ball rolling.

Sincerely, Newton

Jay jerked open the door and stepped out into the cool spring afternoon. He slowly slid down the body of his truck and leaned against it, reading the letter again and again until it burned in his mind. He looked out over the large field that once belonged to his daddy, his grandfather, and his great-grandfather before them. He straightened his cap, stood up, and ran and jumped the ditch to the land that would soon be his. He lay down in the freshly plowed dirt and smelled the sweetness of the turned soil. He cried for his mom and dad, thinking of his father's slow demise and of his mother staring vacantly at the land she would never again own.

As the sun started to set over the Soul River swamp, Jay saw Sonia and Jay, Jr. walking down the road toward him.

"Jay, honey, what in the world is wrong?" Sonia asked when she saw her husband lying in the field.

He pulled himself out of the dirt, jumped across the ditch, handed her the letter, then jumped back and knelt down in the dirt.

He looked at her with tears in his eyes. "Sonia, I'm going to be a farmer."

Sonia looked at him, thinking he was losing his mind. All the stress over the years had finally gotten to him. She read the letter out loud so Jay Jr. could hear.

She looked back at Jay. "This has got to be a

hoax of some sort." Sonia looked back at the letter.

Jay smiled and ran his hands through the dirt, already thinking of what he was going to plant.

Sonia shook her head trying to believe it, but her distrust in the Timrods was greater. "Jay, you know Newton Timrod wasn't right. Everyone in town talked about him. I'm going to call Earl Rivers to be sure this isn't some Timrod bullshit."

She turned and headed back to the house, where she looked up the phone number for the American Legion. Everybody knew where to find Earl Rivers after 5:00 pm.

The bartender passed the phone to Earl. "It's Sonia Sumpter."

Earl took the phone and turned his back to the room. He didn't want anyone to hear their conversation. "Hey, Sonia."

"Mr. Rivers, I'm sorry to bother you after hours but we got a letter from Newton Timrod today, and it claims he is giving our land back to us. Is this so?"

Earl stepped deeper into the hall, away from the bar. "Sonia, Newton is giving the land back to you and Jay. It *is* true, but it will take some time. At least a year for the Will to go through probate.

But, yes to your question, you will have the land back, every acre of it."

Earl waited for her to respond. The other end was silent for a few seconds. "Are you there, Sonia?"

"Yes, I'm here. But why?"

Earl leaned against the wall. "Because Newton knew it was the right thing to do."

10

Dinner Stop

Monday had been bad enough with Newton killing himself and with all the excitement surrounding the tragedy, but Tuesday had also turned into a horrible nightmare. The news spread around town at a quick pace. Finally, the folks of Riverton had something exciting to gossip about.

As for Ella, it was a day of ups and downs, and it was beginning to overwhelm her. She never stooped to crying in front of anyone, but she was about to lose her wits. Ella sat in the car waiting for Langford to finish a call. He paced back and forth in front of the car, one hand in his pocket and the other with the cell phone at his ear, speaking to someone beyond her earshot. She watched him closely, trying to figure out his age. He was a handsome man, especially with his gray hair and blue eyes. *Langford has to be close to my age*, she thought.

He got back in the car, and turned to Ella. "Well, it seems that Angel is going to stay with her parents tonight. Is there a hotel in Riverton where I can get a room?"

Ella took a deep breath and gripped the steering wheel. "There is, but I will not have you stay in that dump of a hotel. You'll be my guest at my house. I have plenty of space."

"Well, thank you, Ella. I'll need to go by Bitty's and get my bag out of Angel's car. Do you mind?"

"Not at all. It's on the way home." She started the car and pulled out of Earl River's parking lot.

Langford watched as the small town passed by and melted into farmland. He couldn't help but think of Newton and the demons he had struggled with. *Small southern towns, so many dark secrets.*

He reflected back to the first time he consulted with Newton's therapist, who wasn't sure if the therapy for depression was helping without prescribing medication. The therapist suggested that medication might help, and with that suggestion, Newton requested a referral to Dr. Langford Wallace's practice on the first floor of the same building.

Ella turned onto Sandy Creek Road, a right turn just before crossing the Wilson Timrod bridge spanning the Soul River. She and Langford traveled a few miles toward Sandy Creek, the beauty of the setting sun across the Soul River swamp was breathtaking.

Ella pointed out a road that went down to the river. "That's where my husband accidently shot himself, fell into the river and drowned."

"Sorry, Ella, I can't imagine how horrible that accident must have been for you. How old were you?"

"Twenty-two. Too young to be a widow." A sadness reflected across her face.

"I agree." Langford noticed how high the river seemed to be and commented to Ella, "Does the river often come so close to the road?"

"The old Soul is in its springtime freshet."

Langford nodded that he understood. "I see. I've heard this term before."

She smiled with pride at her knowledge about the river. "It begins in the mountains with the heavy rains north of us. It's really a beautiful time when it backs up and covers the floor of the swamp, nourishing the cypress and tupelo trees and other swamp plants."

He couldn't help but smile, listening to her explanation.

Sandy Creek came into view, and the first place Langford saw was the Barbeque Hut. "I'm starving,

Ella. How about we stop for dinner?"

"Oh, Lord, no. I can't go to the Barbeque Hut," she said, shaking her head.

"Sure you can. Pull in. It will be good." He motioned with his hand to the parking lot, which was almost full.

Ella reluctantly turned in, parked, and faced him. "Langford, you don't understand. I am a Timrod. I can't go in there." She shook her head. "People will talk."

"So, let them talk." Langford jumped out of the car, took off his coat and tie and tossed them into the back seat. He walked around and opened her door, reached in and took her hand.

"Come on, Ella." He was thinking he might have to pry her out of the driver's seat. "Let's go, Ms. Timrod and get some gossip stirring," he said with a laugh.

Ella conceded and grabbed her purse with a death grip. Langford walked close beside her for support. He knew this was a big step for her to venture out of her comfort zone, which was very small.

The smell of wood burning from the pits around back wafted through the air.

When they walked through the door, a silence fell over the dining room. Everyone turned and looked in disbelief. Blacks and whites couldn't believe their eyes. Ella Timrod had just walked through the front door of the Barbeque Hut.

Ella felt way out of place, but not Langford. He felt right at home.

Latisha Whitmore approached them with a big smile and a couple of menus. Then a voice from the corner of the room called out.

"Ella, over here." Ella looked, and sure enough, it was Bitty. "Y'all come on over here. We've been waiting for you," Bitty called out with a wave.

Very quickly, Ella realized this was a setup. "You had this planned all along, didn't you?"

"Well, sort of; Angel helped," Langford admitted. He escorted her to the table.

The group all stood as Ella approached. She knew she would have to act graciously for Bitty. Langford pulled her chair out, and they all sat down.

An uncomfortable silence fell on the group, and Stanley spoke up. "Well, Ms. Timrod, what do you think about my little girl?"

"Well, Stanley, Angel's not a little girl any-more, and I'm as proud of her as you and Bitty must be. I always knew she had the ability to do anything she wanted, if she applied herself."

She turned to Angel. "I guess my assumptions of you and Newton were incorrect, Angel. I apologize."

Angel smiled at Ella and put her arm around her, hoping to send a message that it was okay to drop the small town uppity persona.

"Ms. Timrod, we're all good friends and family around this table." Angel smiled at her mother and winked.

Bitty knew Ella was struggling, so she chimed up. "I'm hungry. Let's order some food so everyone can go home and get some rest."

After dinner, Langford volunteered to drive. Ella relented, since darkness had engulfed the road home. The headlights illuminated the edges of Sandy Creek Road as they drove along the foggy Soul River swamp. The reflection of animal eyes alerted Langford to a deer standing near the shoulder of the road.

Ella spoke up. "Watch yourself now, you're not in downtown Charleston."

"I'm used to roads very similar to this where I live. My house is actually outside of the city in an isolated area," Langford said to assure Ella that he knew what he was doing.

When they crossed the bridge named for Ella's father, Langford took the opportunity to mention him, fishing for any kind of comment that would open the door to her life with her father. "Wilson Timrod must have been an influential man in Soul County."

A long silence fell over the two. Then she spoke. "My father was a bad man. People didn't know his dark side. He had his cronies who

followed him around like beaten down dogs. He hurt a lot of people, including his own family." She said nothing else.

Langford spoke in a calm and understanding tone. "Ella, I know quite a bit about your father and the cruelties that went on. Newton and I spent a lot of time talking about him. I'm a good listener if you need to talk."

Langford pulled into her carport and turned off the ignition. He put his arm on the back of Ella's seat and watched her in silence. She sat looking off into the darkness. He hoped she would respond or say anything to his offer.

She tucked her purse under her arm, opened the car door and stepped out into the night. "Well, let's get in the house and get you settled in a bed-room."

Langford got the message that she wasn't going to say another word about her father, at least not tonight.

11

Houseguest

Ella escorted Langford to one of the guest rooms on the main floor of the house. He laid his bag on the bed and looked for a place to hang his clothes. He spied a gorgeous cherry wood armoire, opened the doors, and the smell of old furniture caught his senses. It wasn't an unpleasant smell, but it was clear the furniture had been around a while. He hung his suits up and left the doors open to let the inside breathe a little. Every piece in the room was made from cherry wood. It appeared to be all handmade and was exquisite work.

He heard a soft tap on the door.

"Langford, excuse me. I have your bath towels, soap, and a robe. The bathroom is across the hall, so you'll need the robe."

"Please, come in." He held his arms out in awe. "I'm just admiring the furnishings."

Ella laid her bundle on the end of his bed. "Yes, it is a nice set. Handmade many years ago when we had more artisans making furniture for the wealthy.

Curious, he asked, "Who was the woodworker?" He walked over to inspect the chest of drawers closely.

She shrugged her shoulders. "I don't know. It was made before my birth and is well over eighty years old or even much older."

Langford stepped to the window, pulled back the drapes, and looked out into the night. "Do you mind turning the light off? Please, Ella, just for a few moments." He motioned to the lamp.

Ella immediately wondered what he was up to. She turned the lamp off and stood in the room's darkness, waiting to see where this was heading.

Langford spoke softly. "Come here, Ella. I want you to see this." He pushed both sides of the curtains back.

"What in the world do you want me to see? It's dark here, and I might trip." Her voiced was edged with panic.

He walked over to her and took her hand, leading her to the window. "Look what's peeking over the Soul River swamp." he pointed his finger toward the bright ball of light.

"I've seen a moonrise before." She reached over and turned the lamp back on.

He hoped to get more of a positive reaction from her, but Ella's stoicism persisted.

Langford dug around in his bag and pulled out a bottle of Knob Creek bourbon. "Come on, Ella, let's sit on your front porch, watch the moonrise, and have a nightcap."

"I don't drink spirits."

She was lying, but she wouldn't have anyone think she had a drinking problem. She usually had a small glass of bourbon every night before bedtime while she read her book.

Langford looked her straight in the eye. "I know you have a drink every night. I know more about you than you think." He laughed and motioned for her to follow him.

Feeling tired and defeated, she silently cursed Newton for sharing all of his morbid past with this man, and the more she talked with Langford, the more she discovered he knew her past.

Nevertheless, she followed him down the hall to the kitchen, where he started opening cabinets.

She watched him rummage around her tidy kitchen. "Can I help you find something, Langford?" she asked, disgusted.

He turned and smiled. "Yes, a couple of tumblers for our bourbon."

Ella stepped into the dining room and returned with two Waterford crystal cocktail glasses of perfect weight and size. "If we're going to have a nightcap, we may as well do it in style. Since you know so much about me, I'll join you."

"Great." Langford beamed with excitement, opened the bottle, and started to pour a little into her glass.

Ella found it exhausting to be around such a positive and happy person this late in the evening. Usually, she would be sitting alone reading.

She found her wool shawl, and the two adjourned to the front porch. The moon had risen higher in the night sky, and the land surrounding the farm reflected a silvery glow.

The smell of spring and the land waking from its winter sleep flooded Langford's senses. Far across the freshly plowed fields, he could make out the Soul River swamp, a dark and foreboding place.

Ella sipped her bourbon and gently rocked in her chair. Langford was silent, admiring the beauty of the night.

The two remained quiet for some time before Ella asked.

"Do you mind me asking your age, Langford?" She turned to see his expression in reaction to her forward question.

Langford only smiled and took a sip of his bourbon. "Seventy-six. And you, Ella?"

"Well, I guess it's fair that I tell you, but I'm sure you already know," she replied sarcastically. "Seventy-eight."

She continued her questioning. "What sort of relationship did you have with Newton?" she asked softly.

Langford shifted in his chair. "It's a long story, but I'd rather wait. How about tomorrow morning? We'll have an in-depth conversation about it. Let's enjoy our drink, the quiet of the night, and remember Newton.

The two sat staring off into the moonlit night until Ella'd had enough. She stood up, and said her goodnight. "Please, lock the door behind you. I'm usually up early. Have a restful night, Langford."

She disappeared into the house. He sipped his bourbon, knowing that, in the morning, what he had to tell Ella wouldn't be taken graciously.

Ella stood in the kitchen's dark, washing her drink glass, staring out the window into the night. She wondered what the rest of her week would unfold. She carefully dried the glass and returned it to its proper place in the china cabinet.

She found herself at the bottom of the grand staircase, staring at the portrait of her psychopathic father. The horrid memories gushed through her mind. *Why did he have to be so mean and abusive?* The eyes of the old man looked down on her. Even though it was only a portrait, it still fired up the fear and hatred she held in her heart for him.

Ella turned on a couple of lights so Langford could see his way around, then climbed the stairs to her room, hoping she would be able to sleep with the nightmares.

12

The Revelation

Before climbing into bed, Langford had opened a window to allow fresh air to clear the stuffy room, the curtains moved slowly from an almost nonexistent breeze, and the room remained stuffy throughout the night.

The smell of bacon frying and fresh coffee brewing woke Langford from his deep sleep.

His back hurt from the strange bed, and he had a bit of a headache. He stretched his stiff body and moaned. *The furniture may be fine antiques, but the mattress has a lot to be desired.* He slowly sat up on the edge of the bed and ran his hands over his face, trying to shake off the night's sleep.

Gazing out the window, Langford noticed a thick fog clung to the fields, waiting for the sun to burn it off. He reached for a glass of water on the bedside table and drank it down.

One bourbon hadn't done the trick last night, so he had lingered on the porch, thinking of how he was going to deliver the news to Ella in the morning. It was a daunting task, even though Langford was a confident man. He had to be in his line of work as a medical doctor. He was never timid and felt that being direct and seeing that patients go to the right specialist was important.

Well known in Charleston for his empathetic bedside manner, Langford was willing to go the extra mile to help those who walked through his office door. He was more like a country doctor living in a big city, where he was known and admired by all the other doctors at the Medical University. Langford was asked, on occasion, to lecture on eldercare, especially concerning those who had no family and were in nursing homes until the end of their time.

Langford picked up the robe and other items Ella had left for him, grabbed his shaving kit and headed across the hall. He was taken aback by the old but extremely clean bathroom. An ancient, white porcelain clawfoot tub was fitted with a showerhead running from a single pipe at one end. The shower curtain was attached to a circular rod and opened at the other end of the tub.

Instead of showering, he decided to take a soak. He pushed the curtain away and placed the plug in the drain, praying there would be plenty of hot water to fill the bath.

Langford slid down into the tub until his body was completely submerged, except for his knees poking up. Steam rose in the cool air and fogged up the mirror over the sink. It was comforting on his old back. He took a deep breath and searched his mind on how to start his conversation with Ella. *She needs to know Newton's wishes, and I, too, want her to know.*

After his bath and shave, he dressed in a cotton shirt and jeans. Langford combed his wet hair back and put it in a ponytail. He liked having his hair long. It was a carryover from the sixties. He checked himself in the mirror and then proceeded to the kitchen, where, to his surprise, he found Ella, Bitty and Angel having coffee.

Ella glanced at her watch. "Glad you decided to join us. I'll get you a cup. Coffee is over on the counter." She motioned to the Mr. Coffee and handed him a cream-colored Wedgewood cup.

He eyed the dainty cup in his hand and would have preferred a nice mug but kept that to himself.

She read his mind, opened a cabinet and pulled out a large cheap mug. "Does this suit you better, Langford?"

"Yes, very nice, thank you."

He smiled at Angel sitting across the room at the kitchen table. She rolled her eyes and smiled back knowingly.

Ella picked up an egg. "Would you care for breakfast?"

Langford thought for a moment. "I think I'll just have toast, but not right now. Have a seat, Ella. We need to talk."

Ella filled her cup, added a little sugar and cream and sat directly across from him with Bitty on one side of her and Angel on the other. "Okay, I'm all ears."

Langford took a couple of sips of coffee. "Excellent coffee, ladies."

He put his cup down and looked Ella straight in the eyes.

"Ella, I have a story to tell you about a beautiful, young girl from Charleston. Her name was Maggie."

Langford closed his eyes, and the memory of his sweet mother raced through his mind. She had been a beautiful woman, and even after all the years gone by, he missed her.

"When Maggie was seventeen, she had great plans to go to college and become a teacher, but her life dream was interrupted. Her parents were well-known, blue blood Charlestonians. I mean South of Broad bunch, if you understand the term."

"Of course, Langford, I know what you mean," Ella laughed.

He continued. "Maggie's father was a banker and investor in the tobacco industry. One day, he brought a guest home to stay for the weekend. This man was one of the major tobacco farmers in South Carolina. He noticed the beautiful Maggie and engaged her in conversation, ingratiating himself with her father by telling him how impressed he was with her intellect. He managed to gain Maggie's confidence while there, but behind the friendly face was the mind of a predator."

Langford took a deep breath and sipped his coffee, still making eye contact with Ella.

"On his last night as their guest, they had a big dinner, where a lot of wine and spirits were enjoyed. Even Maggie was allowed a glass of champagne. She excused herself right after dinner and went to bed."

Langford paused and looked at Bitty and Angel as if to get a little strength from them to go on. "After midnight, everyone else went to bed with plenty of drink in their bellies. The wealthy guest saw his opportunity to take what he wanted. He slipped into Maggie's room and sexually assaulted her. He raped her. Afterward, he told her that if she breathed a word of it to anyone, it could ruin her father's business and that no one would believe her anyway."

Ella's hand started to tremble as she picked up her coffee cup and took a sip. "I'm not going to like the ending of this story, am I, Langford?" she said with trepidation.

He leaned back in his chair, and, with a serious look, he continued with his story. "After the guest had been gone a couple of months, the young Maggie found out she was pregnant. To save face, her parents shipped her off to a private hospital to have the child. The plan was to give it up for adoption. Anyone inquiring about Maggie was told she was ill and needed special care."

Langford got up and refilled his cup. He walked behind Ella and put his hand on her shoulder. "Ella, I am that child, your half brother."

Ella's face dropped into her hands. "Oh, God."

She stood up abruptly and walked out the back door to her flower garden, leaving the three wondering about her present state of mind.

Langford watched from the window. "Give her a few minutes alone so she can process what she's heard. I, myself, would certainly need some time."

"She'll figure out that I told Momma." Angel voiced her concern.

The back door opened, and Ella appeared. "Tell me more. I want to know everything."

She looked at Bitty. "Did you know, Bitty?"

Bitty shook her head as if to say no. "Ella, Angel told me last night. I promise I never knew before that. This is why we were here early this morning, to be with you when Langford told you."

Ella sat back down, as did Langford. She turned her head away from him. "You realize this is opening a Pandora's box, and I'd just as soon not let those demons out."

"Ella, I do understand," Langford nodded gently.

Bitty took Ella's hand and squeezed it tightly. "Ella, we've been friends for a long time. I love you, and I'm here for you."

Langford continued with his story. "My mother's Charleston family was in a frenzy to keep this unwanted child a secret, so my mother was sent away to stay at a girls' home in Charlotte. When my mother gave birth to me, her parents intended to put me up for adoption, but Maggie, having turned eighteen, wouldn't have any part of it. I was her baby, and she was determined to keep me.

"She stayed with nuns and raised her baby boy. Maggie went back to school, became a teacher and married a wonderful young man, who, as far as I'm concerned, was the only father I ever knew. They had two more children, my brother and sister, who still live in the Charlotte area."

Ella put a hand up. "Wait a minute."

Then she asked the question that Langford knew was coming. "Why should I believe this story?"

He smiled at her. "Ella, when I was eighteen, my mother was diagnosed with cancer. She was very ill and dying. I was getting ready to go off to college and not real happy about leaving my dad and younger siblings to care for her.

The day before I had to leave, she asked to see me at her bedside. She told me who my real father was and what happened. She showed me the letters she had written to him asking for help after my birth. She also had his letter threatening a restraining order if she tried to contact him again.

My mother told me everything about the horrible assault. Years later, she did some poking around and found out a lot about the Timrod family. She had it all written down and passed it over to me that day." Pausing, he added, "I made a promise to myself that I would learn as much as I could about this terrible man, who is my blood father.

"So, how did you get to know Newton?"

Langford took a deep breath. "Well, because of my mother and my own curiosity, I knew a lot about you, Newton and the history of the rest of the family, your older brothers dying in the war and your poor sister suffering here in this house. Then, the time came when I decided not to pursue it any more. I had a medical practice to run. A family of my own, and I needed to get on with my life and work.

"One day, years later, I received a call from one of the clinical psychologists in the same building as my office. He had a patient who needed medication for depression. That patient specifically requested to see me for the medication.

"The next day, I picked up the file off the nurse's desk. I glanced at the name before walking into the examining room, and I couldn't believe my eyes. I knew that when I walked through the door, I would be looking at my half brother. I thought that was going to be an interesting conversation. I briefly considered giving the file to my partner, but something told me to go through that door and meet Newton Timrod.

"I was so nervous, my hands started to shake a little. I felt like I was going to say something stupid like, 'Hey, brother, how are you?' Langford laughed, took a big sip of coffee and looked straight at Ella. "But Newton beat me to it."

Ella was dumbfounded. She became angry at Langford and accused him of trying to ruin her family name and even take her inheritance.

"This is nonsense, Dr. Wallace, and before you say another word, you need to produce those letters and some sort of scientific proof."

Langford looked at Bitty and Angel. "I thought this would be difficult." He shook his head as if agreeing with himself. "I'll be right back."

Langford disappeared down the hall.

Ella twitched in her seat. "Bitty, do you believe what you're hearing?"

Bitty nodded. "Yes, Ella, I do. I don't think this man needs your money or any part of this place. He wants you to know the truth. I believe that is all."

"Ms. Timrod . . ." Angel started to chime in, but was interrupted.

"Angel, please call me Ella. You're old enough to do that now."

"Okay, Ella. Newton and Langford have been close for years. I know that Newton wanted you to know your brother. There's lots more you're going to learn over the next few days."

Ella looked surprised at Angel's comment. "What do you mean?"

"It's not my place to tell you." Angel got up and walked down the hall to find Langford.

In a few minutes, they returned, and Langford laid the letters out on the table.

"Here's your proof, Ella, along with the DNA test Newton and I had done to prove that we are brothers. Newton said you would want this sort of evidence. I'll be on the porch with my coffee when you're ready to continue our conversation."

Langford quietly sat in his rocker taking in the beauty of the spring morning. He studied the three dilapidated tobacco barns and thought of how deeply the tobacco industry had adversely affected so many people.

He left the porch and wandered across the street to the old barns, figuring Ella was still fuming over the news of him being her half brother. He felt she would eventually come to her senses and let him finish with the conversation.

Looking at the oak tree Newton plowed into revealed only a small scar. Langford could see very little evidence of the commotion of emergency vehicles immediately following the wreck.

With hands in his pockets, he walked around the barns staring at the ground in deep thought. *Why am I doing this for Ella? She is so obstinate. Newton warned me.* Langford kicked at an old piece of metal lying in the dust and wondered how long it had been there.

The sound of a door slamming got his attention. It was Ella, and she was coming toward him with a purpose. Briskly walking across the road, she didn't even look to see if a car might be approaching.

He watched her come closer, clutching the papers he left for her to read. Ella stopped about ten feet away from Langford. Shaking the papers at him, she spoke sharply. "Okay, Langford, where do we go from here?"

Unable to go on, Ella broke down in tears.

He rushed to her side and put his arm around her. "What we do, Ella, is enjoy our lives as brother and sister."

Through her sobbing, she spilled what was really troubling her. "But you're going to want part of my land and the house. It's all I have, and all I know. It's my life . . ."

Langford let out a big laugh. "Ella, I don't want any of your property or any part of that house. All I want is for you to know the truth. It's what Newton wanted. He loved you even though you two avoided each other like the plague."

Langford escorted her back to the house, where they sat on the porch until she gained her composure.

"What else do I need to know?" She wiped the tears off her cheeks.

Langford rocked back in his chair and steepled his fingers to his lips. "Quite a lot, Ella," he replied.

Sally Glass

13

The Killing Grounds

Mary Lou Reese was a pretty fourteen-year-old blonde with green eyes. She came from good stock for looks, but from the poor side of town, and if you were impoverished in Soul County, good looks didn't matter. Her life was relegated to hard work; trying to earn enough money to help her mother pay the bills. Mary Lou's father had died when the tractor he was driving turned over, crushing him. Her two younger siblings weren't old enough to work, so it fell into her lap to bring home extra cash.

One summer, she managed to get a job tying tobacco on the Timrod farm. The boys on the farm worked the fields picking the leaves, loading up a drag sled and delivering the sled to the barn, where the Negro women and Mary Lou would climb onto the stacked up leaves and start tying. Mary Lou would take a bundle of sticky green leaves in her small hands, using another leaf to wrap around the ends of the bundle, and then drape it over a long stick to be hung in the rafters of the curing barn. She was a fast worker and the only white girl. There were a few white boys who worked the fields, but for the most part Wilson Timrod perferred Negro help.

Hanging the tobacco laden sticks took strength and agility. Tobias Williams and another young Negro boy performed this feat with grace and speed. The two spent most of their days in the rafters of the curing barns. It was hot, sticky, dirty work.

Tobias sat on one of the cross beams watching Mary Lou wipe the sweat from her neck. He knew he didn't have a chance with Mary Lou, since his skin didn't match hers, but his dreams were often occupied by her beautiful blond hair and green eyes. Mary Lou was friendly and talkative, but she knew enough to keep her distance.

When there was a lull between sleds coming in, Tobias and Mary Lou would sit just inside the open door of the barn, waiting for the next sled. That was their moment to talk about dreams of a future away from Soul County. Tobias wanted to go to college and study law. He had a better chance of getting out than she did. Tobias's parents were hardworking folks and insisted that he keep up his grades. Mary Lou, on the other hand, lacked a good education, and the demands of her mother and siblings didn't leave her much time to study or have friends.

Chainy Williams, Tobias's grandfather, had worked on the farm for many years and was in charge of tending the fires in the barns. He was old, and that was about all he was capable of doing. He slept in a makeshift room nearby.

Chainy walked into the barn looking for his grandson. "Tobias, where you boy?"

Tobias watched from high up in the rafters, trying not to laugh as his grandfather searched the barn for the wiley boy. Tobacco dust from above was falling all over him.

"Tobias, I know you're hiding up in here. Yo' momma wants you home. School starts tomorrow."

When Tobias heard this, he knew he'd better stop playing and get home. "Okay, Grandpa, I'm headed home, but I want to tell Mary Lou goodbye."

Chainy looked at him crossly. "You leave that white girl alone. All it'll do is get you in trouble. Now get. People in Sandy Creek are already gossiping too much about how you two sit and talk."

After work every day, Mary Lou walked across the road to the Timrod's garage to wash her hands and face at the water spigot. Mr. Timrod parked his Cadillac next to the spigot. He would watch her from his home office window. She had no idea he was spying on her. Wilson Timrod had been watching Mary Lou all summer, planning his crime and waiting. It disgusted him to see her talking to the black boy. He was sure they were up to something. He was waiting for just the right moment when all the workers had left. Bitty and Ella had gone into Riverton to shop. Newton was in his room reading. The moment was now. Not a soul to see him snatch her up and go.

The day was waning, and Mary Lou wanted to collect her pay and catch a ride home. She usually jumped in the back of a pickup with a couple of the white field hands. She stood up after washing her face and immediately felt a hand on the back of her neck.

"Get in the car and lay down in the passenger side," a gruff voice whispered in her ear.

"Mr. Timrod, what are you doing? I don't understand." Mary Lou shook with fear.

"Get in the car and lay down on the floorboard now," he said hatefully.

Across the road, hidden from sight, Tobias watched Wilson Timrod throw Mary Lou in his car.

He didn't understand what was going on, but somehow he knew not to show himself. He watched Wilson Timrod drive off with Mary Lou in the Cadillac, then ran back to where his grandpa was stacking oak wood for the fires.

"Grandpa, Mr. Timrod pushed Mary Lou into his car and drove off. What do you think he's going to do with her?"

Chainy was getting irritated with Tobias. "Boy, now you listen to me," Chainy pointed his finger at Tobias. "What Wilson Timrod does with a white girl ain't none of mine nor your business. Now you take my pickup and get home before your momma and daddy kills both of us. I'm too old to be worrying about any of the Timrods or their white women."

Tobias looked down at the ground. "Yes, sir."

From an upstairs window, Newton was shocked at what he saw. His father was roughly handling one of the workers. He watched the car drive away, and he knew deep inside what would happen.

Wilson Timrod's dark blue Cadillac hummed along the blacktop, then turned down a dirt road and disappeared into the deep recesses of the Soul River swamp. Darkness was setting in. The only light to be seen was far away, coming from the Sumpter farmhouse porch.

Mary Lou was frantic with fear. She had no idea what was about to happen to her. "What are you going to do to me, Mr. Timrod?"

"Shut up, you little whore," he said angrily.

"Whore? I'm not a whore. I've never been with a boy. All I've done is work and help my mother," she said through sobs and tears.

The car came to a stop. He sat and listened to Mary Lou crying. "Would you please shut up, you little slut. I've seen you talking to that nigger boy."

He was beginning to get worked up. The meanness in his soul began to reveal the true monster in Wilson Timrod.

He opened the door and got out of the car, leaving Mary Lou crying on the floor of the front seat. It seemed like an eternity before her door opened. All she saw was Wilson Timrod standing half naked in the grass. He pulled her out of the car and beat her with his fists. Once she was out cold, he stripped her and raped her.

After he finished, he dragged her nude body to the edge of the swamp. He had beaten her badly and figured death would come soon, but he held her face underwater to help it along. Finally she stopped breathing. He washed his hands at the water's edge and stared at Mary Lou's dead body.

"That was real good, honey. Hope you enjoyed it as much as I did."

He laughed and looked around to be sure no one was watching. He dressed, drove into town, stopped at the American Legion and had a drink with some local cronies. Not a soul suspected that they were in the presence of a psychopath.

Mary Lou's mother called the sheriff when she didn't arrive home that evening. He came out and gave her the old song and dance that Mary Lou most likely ran away or was with a friend.

Her mother protested, but her lowly status in Soul County meant nothing to the sheriff.

"Joanne, if she's not home in a couple of days, call me back, but I bet she has run off. She'll be back."

Dub Henson had been sheriff of Soul County for years. He was your typical paid off, corrupt sheriff. He was lazy and didn't do any poking around until he consulted with certain higher powers in the county. One of those individuals happened to be Wilson Timrod, himself.

The next morning, the sheriff's wife had served him up his favorite breakfast of hog head cheese, grits, and eggs with a side of white bread toast. He had just finished, when his phone rang.

The wall phone was down the hall, and he took his time getting to it. "Sheriff Henson speaking."

"Sheriff, this is Charlie Jordan." The phone was quiet for a few seconds, then Charlie cleared his throat.

"What's up, Charlie? Are you and your brother in trouble again?"

"Naw, Sheriff, my news is worse than that."

"Well, tell me, boy," he said impatiently.

"Me and Tommy were over on the backside of the Timrod land near the swamp, just beating around this morning. You know, off County Road 316?"

"I know where you're talking about now, get to the point." He said angrily.

"We walked back into the swamp, and we found Mary Lou Reese's body. She'd been beat up pretty damn bad. She's dead. No sign of life. We ain't told not a soul. I left Tommy hiding in the swamp to keep watch over her until I could get you."

"Where are you calling from?"

"Taylor's store. The pay phone."

"I'm on my way. I'll pick you up."

He grabbed his hat and pistol. "I got a call, Louise. I'll see you later."

The dirt road back into the river swamp had been well-traveled. The sheriff figured it would be impossible to determine the age of any of the tracks.

Tommy popped up out of the weeds where he had been hiding and watching Mary Lou's body.

"Charlie, there ain't been a soul in or out." Tommy's voice shook.

Sheriff Henson crawled out of his patrol car and adjusted his pants that had dropped a bit from sitting in the car. He stepped around anything he thought might be evidence.

Mary Lou's nude body, white as snow, lay face down with her head turned to the side. Her face was swollen and red.

"My God, who in God's green earth would do this?" He turned away from the body.

"I need some help." He put his hand on his hip and thought for a moment.

"Charlie, take my car to the Timrod place and

get Wilson Timrod to come and help us out. Open the trunk and get me the blanket before you go."

Charlie found the old army blanket and handed it to the sheriff, who covered Mary Lou's body.

Wilson Timrod arrived with Chainy sitting in the passenger seat of the farm truck. "You stay in the truck until I need you," he told the old man.

"Yes, sir, Mr. Wilson," Chainy nodded with respect. Deep inside he despised the wealthy, arrogant bastard.

Wilson Timrod wore mud boots, a hunting jacket and leather gloves to hide the bruises on his knuckles. He was dressed a little too nice for the situation at hand. He adjusted his field hat and strolled to where Sheriff Henson stood over Wilson's wicked work from the night before.

"Dub, who in the world would do this?" Wilson asked, shaking his head.

"Wilson, I don't know. Surely it had to be some transient passing through. I don't know of a single person from around these parts who would do such a terrible thing." Dub shook his head.

"Her momma reported her missing last night, but I figured she ran away or was with friends."

Wilson Timrod studied the ground around her body to make sure he hadn't left any evidence. Even though he was pretty sure he hadn't, his thought was to get her moved and fast.

"We need to get her out of here. This is just awful. I can't bear to see her like this. She was a good worker and a sweet girl. Everyone thought the world of her. At least get her over to the funeral home, Sheriff, so you can tell her momma."

Wilson thought for a moment as he worked his magic with Dub. "Let's wrap her up in a blanket and lay her in the bed of my truck. I can't stand seeing her in that muck any longer." Wilson grimaced.

"What about calling the coroner?" Dub asked.

"I'll take responsibility for making this decision," Wilson said with authority.

The two part-time deputies, who had just arrived, helped lift her onto the bed of the truck. Chainy sat quietly in the passenger side, turning a little to see what he could of the covered girl.

"I'll take her right over to the funeral home and call the coroner while you go and find her mother," Wilson directed.

Wilson Timrod knew he had to move her from

the scene of the crime before the coroner saw her. He knew he was breaking the law by doing this, but he would play dumb and emotional about her young body all exposed to the elements. The coroner was a good friend of his anyway, so not much would be said about it.

Later that day, Tobias pulled his grandpa's truck up to the row of tobacco barns. He had just finished his first day back at school and had come to relieve Chainy so he could go home, eat and rest up for the coming night. "Grandpa, you here?"

Chainy appeared from inside one of the barns holding a piece of oak wood. He had a hard time hiding his distress. It had been a terrible day, and his concern for his grandson had left him a nervous wreck. "How was school today?"

"Oh, it was good. I like all my teachers." Tobias smiled.

"Tobias, when you left here yesterday, where'd you go, boy?"

Tobias looked confused and thought his grandpa was losing his mind. "I went straight home, like you said."

"Did you see anybody on the road going home?" Chainy asked.

"Yes, sir. I gave old Billy and Justice a ride to Sandy Creek."

"Did you see anything else after you came to me and told me about Mr. Timrod taking Mary Lou in his car yesterday evening?" Chainy questioned.

Tobias thought about it for a moment. "No, Grandpa. It bothered me to see her get in his car, but I took your advice and let it go. Just figured it was none of my business."

Tobias was confused by all the questions. "What's wrong?"

Chainy pulled him around behind the barn. "Boy, you listen to me now. They found Mary Lou's body on the edge of the river swamp this morning. She had been beaten to death. Don't know what else was done to her."

Chainy studied his grandson.

Tobias sat down on one of the tobacco sleds. "I knew something was wrong with her. She looked scared of Mr. Timrod. Did he do this?"

Chainy's heart leaped out of his chest. "You know that dream you have of being an attorney and helping people, your kind of folks, our people? Well, if you want that life, you need to play dumb and keep your mouth shut."

Chainy grabbed Tobias by the shoulders. "You hear what I'm saying to you?"

Tobias's mind wandered back to the day before. He felt a tinge of guilt rise up in his stomach and felt sick, as if he was going to throw up. He looked at his grandpa with watery eyes. "She was such a pretty girl, grandpa. Did Mr. Timrod kill her?"

"Boy, I don't know, and neither do you. Now, do as I say and keep your mouth shut. Get through this year, and you're off to school somewhere out of this hell hole. Then you'll never have to touch another leaf or stick of tobacco."

Tobias wiped his eyes trying to push what he had seen out of his mind. He knew deep in his heart that Wilson Timrod had done this to Mary Lou.

Chainy sat down beside him. "Now, go home and stay home. Have your momma bring me some dinner. I'll have a talk with Mr. Timrod about getting someone else to help me. I'll tell him your mother wants you buried in the books this year. Now get home."

Tobias drove away worrying about his grandpa, his future and mostly about the pretty, green-eyed Mary Lou Reese. The trauma of seeing her driven away to her death would never leave him.

For weeks, crazy rumors about Mary Lou Reese were spread around Riverton. Some slandered her viciously, all because she was poor. Others said her preference for Negro boys got her killed. The Klan didn't approve of such activities, and some folks strongly felt it was the Klan who had her killed.

Sheriff Henson talked to everyone who saw her the day she went missing. Wilson Timrod pretty much told the truth with lies interwoven in his tale. He said he paid her and last saw her washing her face and hands at his spigot before walking off down the road. Maybe she was robbed of her pay and left for dead.

Tobias was questioned, but he had witnesses to corroborate his story. One lady in Riverton told the sheriff she saw a stranger in a beat up car in town on the same day Mary Lou disappeared. Another man saw the same car. One witness said it was black and the other said beige. That was about all Sheriff Henson had to go on.

Weeks turned into months, months into years, and the case went into the back of a file cabinet. All that remained of Mary Lou's memory was a small headstone that some kindly townsfolk purchased for her.

Tobias spent four years at South Carolina State. He was president of the student body and graduated Magna Cum Laude. His greatest achievement was being accepted into Harvard Law School.

Even with all his accolades, Tobias still carried the memory of watching Wilson Timrod drive off with Mary Lou Reese in his car, never to see her again. She was a sweet, innocent victim. Tobias promised her in his prayers that he would reveal Wilson Timrod and make it right. But first, he needed to become the best attorney he could be.

Chainy lived long enough to see his grandson graduate from Harvard. He died shortly after, at almost one hundred years old. He carried secrets about Wilson Timrod to his grave. No one would ever know what Chainy held onto for most of his life. It was a time when a black man kept his mouth shut and did his job. Tobias always felt his grandfather knew more than he let on to others. Chainy would play the old man who was forgetful and clumsy, but Tobias knew better.

Sheriff Henson ate enough fried food to kill a bear, and it finally caught up with him one day. He dropped dead while climbing the front steps of the county courthouse.

Wilson Timrod suffered a stroke a year after he murdered Mary Lou. He was bedridden for the rest of his miserable life. His son, Newton, and daughter, Ella, took over managing the farm. It was now Wilson Timrod's time as a bedridden invalid to suffer for his actions.

14

Witness

After the traumatic morning when she learned that Langford was her half brother, Ella retreated to her room. The stress of trying to take in too much information left her exhausted. She tried to get a little more sleep, but her mind kept running in circles.

She finally gave up trying to sleep and went down to the kitchen. There she found a note from Bitty indicating she had gone to visit cousins with Angel, and that lunch was ready in the refrigerator.

Ella ate a little, had a cup of coffee, and flipped through her gardening magazine until she couldn't stand the quiet any longer. It was closing in on her.

She needed some sort of distraction. Her thoughts were traveling back to memories she wished not to entertain. She looked out the front door at the afternoon sun. It seemed to linger a little longer than usual, casting long shadows across the yard that changed as the sun slowly eased its way toward setting. Dark would soon close in around Ella's house of horrors.

It was in the dark that Ella experienced her worst trauma. Her mind raced back to her childhood and the unwelcome visitor who often came to her room at night. She would freeze with fear. He always wore a black cloth mask, but she knew who it was despite the mask. Her father molested her over and over into her teen years. She learned to find places to hide in her mind, but her body could not. She pushed the terrifying memories deep inside.

Where is Langford this afternoon? She walked up to his room and heard snoring behind his door. *At least someone can get a little sleep.*

Ella eased out the door and sat alone on the porch. She kept going over and over her conversation with Langford from earlier in the day. In a matter of days, her life had been turned completely upside down. She feared hearing more stories about her past and about the awful things her father did, not only to her but to other people, as well.

The screen door opened, and Langford walked out with two tumblers of bourbon. "Join me, Ella."

She was surprised, since she hadn't heard any stirring inside. "Sure, why not?" she capitulated, reaching for the glass.

"Did you get a bite to eat?" she asked.

"Yes, I did. Bitty prepared a delicious meal. Also had a nice afternoon nap."

Langford sat down on the front steps and stared at the abandoned barns. Rusting machines and old tobacco sleds lay in their final rest, disappearing into the shadows of twilight. "This must have been some kind of operation in its day." He sipped his bourbon.

"It truly was, but my father ran it with an iron fist. Most of the workers were from Sandy Creek, except for a few poor whites, who he referred to as white trash. He watched the operation from his office here in the house.

"When I was a little girl, Mary Kay and I would play dolls here on the front porch. I recall seeing Daddy standing right there." Ella pointed to a large window. "His arms would be crossed. With a cigar in hand, he'd glare at the workers across the road. He saw everything from his office window." She shook her head. "They all feared him."

"When did Bitty start working here?" asked Langford.

"Oh, Bitty came to work when I was 12 or 13.

She and I were the same age, thereabouts. She started working here a few years after my mother died. Bitty helped around the house. She and I spent a lot of time talking and laughing. If my schoolmates came over, I wasn't allowed to talk to Bitty, because she was the Negro help. I would sneak away from my friends and go down to the kitchen to see her." Ella sipped her bourbon and continued.

"Every spring, Bitty and I would plant the vegetable garden. It was sort of my summer project. We grew tomatoes, cucumbers, okra and butter beans. It was a fabulous garden, and it strengthened our friendship. She taught me how to cook, and we canned vegetables, as well. I was amazed at what she could do at such a young age. She has been a dear friend," Ella said with a smile.

Langford stretched his legs out down the steps. "You're blessed to have Bitty for a friend, and her daughter is smart and an excellent nurse practitioner. If not for Newton, who knows what sort of life Angel might have had?"

Ella was curious about Langford. He talked about Newton and Angel but hadn't spoken much about his family. He had mentioned that he and his wife had given Angel a home during her schooling.

"Are you still married?" Ella asked.

"No, I lost Sarah Ann five years ago to cancer," Langford looked away from Ella.

"I'm sorry. Do you mind if I ask what kind of cancer?" she pried.

"Breast cancer. Stage four. We never caught it, not even with the mammograms. It was a fast moving cancer. She was gone within three months of finding it."

"Sorry, Langford."

"Yep, I miss her a great deal. Sarah Ann was the light of my life and of my sons' lives. We were all very close."

"Oh, so you have children?"

"Two sons. My youngest, Tom, is an Air Force fighter pilot stationed at Nellis Air Force Base in Las Vegas. My oldest, Langford, Jr.; we call him Lang, is a pediatrician and lives in Chapel Hill, NC. We got started with family a little late. Sarah Ann was thirty when we had Lang; Tom came along five years later. That's my life."

He looked at Ella and gave her a forced smile. "Shall I get us another?"

Langford stood up, went inside and refreshed their drinks. When he returned, Ella was in the front yard looking over her azaleas.

"Let's walk over to the barns and look at the farm equipment before it gets dark. I like old machines."

Ella picked up her glass, and the two strolled across the road to the barns, where decaying tobacco sleds and tractors seemed to be left where they were last used, covered in dust and cobwebs, ancient relics from a bygone era.

"I can remember when these tractors were brand new." She patted one of the dry rotted tires on the old beast.

Langford brushed the dust off the seat and climbed up on it. "Ella, you could sell these. They're antiques. Except for a little rust and dust, they're in great condition."

"Yes, I know, but I like seeing them sit out here rusting away; sort of what is happening to me," she laughed.

Langford brushed the dust off the name, Farmall. "Definitely a collector's item." He looked at Ella.

"Maybe after we take care of Newton's gala," she said sarcastically.

The two walked from one barn to the next, reliving the past while admiring old machines and large stacks of abandoned tobacco sticks. Ella explained the purpose of all sorts of odd items used in the industry.

"So, tell me about your husband, Ella." Langford asked.

She looked to the ground and then took a deep breath. "Jacob was the love of my life, but he came from a middle class family, and my father couldn't understand how I could love someone he considered to be below me. At least, that's the way he saw it."

Ella turned away from Langford. "Langford, I know my father killed my husband. I just couldn't prove it, and I wouldn't dare go against his word."

Langford put his hand on her shoulder. "Ella, would you like to know the truth? There's an eye-witness to it all."

Ella jerked around. "What do you mean? How could you know this?"

"There's a man you know who witnessed the death of your husband." Langford waited for her response.

"Why didn't he come forward when it happened?" Ella asked.

"Because he was a young Negro man just minding his own business and found himself in the wrong place at the wrong time. During that time in these parts, if he came forward, do you really think people would believe him over Wilson Timrod? They could have turned on him. He did what was best to survive, so he hid. He carried it around for many years, not sharing it with a soul, until Newton started going to the Barbeque Hut for cocktails."

Langford watched Ella put two and two together.

Ella's expression dropped, and the name spilled out of her mouth like soured milk. "Bowman Whitmire!"

Langford acknowledged her with a nod. "Yes, Ella, Bowman Whitmire."

Langford knew that she wouldn't accept Bowman's word so easily, due to his reputation around Sandy Creek and the county. Bowman was known to do some underhanded things, even to his own people in Sandy Creek.

"What else has my brother shared with you and Angel?" She threw back the little bit of bourbon left in her glass.

"Everything he saw and heard. He wrote every bit of it down."

Ella clenched her fists in anger. "Why is this happening to me? Is it necessary to know all the bad my father did, dragging it out so eventually everyone in Riverton will know? People will be whispering behind my back. And the looks, oh my God, the looks I'll get. I won't be able to show myself in Riverton."

Langford tried to comfort her, but she rebuffed his gesture.

"Ella, I'm going to be blunt." Langford tossed his ice cubes out with disgust. "Our father was a psychopath, and people in this town still think he was some kind of god. It's my understanding there's a portrait of him hanging at the county courthouse. Don't you think it's time people really know the truth about who Wilson Timrod was?" He slammed his fist into his open palm, and looked her in the eye.

"There are people who need closure and some sort of peace before they leave this earth. Bowman Whitmire is one. You can either go see him, or he'll come out here to the house. It's up to you, but you owe yourself and Bowman this cleansing opportunity."

Ella turned on Langford. "You are full of hate, as well, Langford Wallace. You want to see Wilson Timrod's reputation ruined for what he did to your mother. Just think, Dr. Wallace, you wouldn't be here if not for our father."

Langford bit his tongue. He was angry, not only about the rape of his mother but also for Newton and all the other victims. Ella had no idea of the true extent of what sort of monster her father really was. Langford felt like the whole bunch needed a psychiatrist assigned to them forever.

Ella crossed the road with Langford close behind. "I'll think about it, " she said.

She opened the screen door and vanished into the house. She went straight to her room and fell across her bed in tears.

Langford found a rocking chair and watched the fading light of day give way to darkness. *What will tomorrow bring?*

Ella sat up. She went to her desk and retrieved the phone book, looked up the Barbeque Hut and dialed the number. The sweet voice of Latisha Whitmire answered.

"Latisha, Ella Timrod. Is Bowman available?"

"Hang on. I'll transfer you to the bar."

"Bowman speaking." He said with his smoker's cough and shortness of breath.

The music in the background and people talking made understanding Bowman difficult for Ella's aged ears.

"Bowman, this is Ella Timrod. I've been told that you have some information I might be interested in."

"Yessum, I do, but only if you want to hear it."

She paused before her next question. "Not that I think you are a dishonest man, but how do I know you're telling the truth?"

"I guess, Ms. Timrod, you don't." Bowman let out several deep coughs.

"I'll see you in the morning. I'll be at your establishment at 9:00."

"Yes, ma'am. I'll have a pot of coffee and some of Latisha's fresh baked sweet rolls. Come around to the side door, it will be open."

Ella hung up. She cringed to the idea of going to Bowman's juke joint alone, but she didn't want anyone hearing what he was going to tell her. Deep down inside, she already knew, but not the details. It would be hard to listen to, but it was important that she find out exactly what went on with her husband and her father in those early morning hours so many years ago.

The next morning Ella informed Langford that she had an appointment, and he would be on his own for a couple of hours. "I would invite you along, but this is something I need to do by myself, if you understand."

"Of course, Ella, I'll be fine. You take your time."

The Buick eased along the main drag in Sandy Creek until the Barbeque Hut came into sight.

"Oh, God, help me with what I am about to hear," she said under her breath.

She pulled around the side of the building. Bowman's son was out back tending to the barbeque pits.

"Good morning, Ms. Timrod," he said with a wave when he saw her.

She parked the car. Taking a deep breath, she exited the car and spoke to the young man. "Good morning, Junior. Is your father inside?"

"Yes ma'am, right through the side door." He smiled at Ella, walked over and opened the door for her.

"Thank you," Ella straightened her stately shoulders, preparing herself.

The smell of stale beer and spirits almost

made her turn around and leave, but she had to hear Bowman's words. Maybe it would help her put this one trauma behind her.

"Good morning, Ms. Ella. Please have a seat." Bowman slowly stood, leaning on his cane with his right hand. He reached out with his left to take her hand, but she wouldn't have any part of shaking hands.

Latisha Bowman appeared with two cups of coffee in beautiful china cups.

Their elegant beauty surprised Ella. "Oh my, what nice cups and saucers."

Latisha smiled. "Yes, ma'am, I thought you would enjoy your coffee in a nicer cup than the ones from the restaurant, and here are a couple of fresh baked cinnamon buns. My specialty."

Ella smiled and thanked her.

Latisha left the room, and a quiet moment fell over Ella and Bowman as they sipped their coffee. It seemed like hours had passed.

Ella finally broke the silence. "So, Bowman, tell me."

Bowman took out a cigar but didn't light it. "I don't smoke anymore, but I like to hold an un-lit cigar. It helps my nerves a lot."

He laughed. "I know my time here is coming to an end. My lungs are shot."

"Sorry to hear that, Bowman," Ella said sincerely.

"Now, about the day you lost your husband." He looked at her across the table.

Ella squirmed nervously in her chair.

He began.

"I had been out all night delivering white liquor for Joe Benson. It was about 3:00 a.m. I was tired. I had finished up and was walking back to Sandy Creek.

"I decided to go up to the river landing to find a place to take a nap. It was cold and I laid down a croker sack and snuggled up into the corner of the Big Cypress wrapping my arms around my shoulders trying to stay warm.

"I had slipped off to sleep for a little while and then just before daybreak I heard a truck Coming down the landing road. The morning sun was burning a thin red line on the horizon, but it was still a little dark. I didn't move just in case it was the law. I heard voices, and I recognized your daddy's voice.

"He and your young man gathered up their hunting gear, put it all in a small boat and paddled out toward the duck blind. By the time they got to the blind the sun had come up more, and I could see the men real good. I peeked around the edge of the tree and watched as your daddy climbed up into the blind. Mr. Timrod turned and told your young man to hand him his shotgun before *he* climbed up."

He did, and as your husband was climbing up, your daddy killed him. Shot him square in the chest. Your young man fell backward. His waders must have filled up with water, and he disappeared below the surface. Then your daddy rowed back to the landing, where he submerged himself to make it look like he had tried to rescue him.

Ella's eyes filled with tears. She searched her purse for a tissue. Bowman handed her a napkin.

"What happened next?"

Bowman continued. "Well, I was scared to death that he would see me behind the tree. I scrunched up between the roots and prayed he didn't see or hear my movement. He stood around for a bit scanning the river and the swamp to be sure no one else was around. Then he got in his truck and drove away, leaving most of his stuff in the boat.

"What did you do, Bowman?" Ella asked.

"When he was out of sight, and I knew he

was really gone, I ran through the swamp and got back to Sandy Creek as fast as I could. I never told a soul. I kept the secret for years, until one night Newton was at the bar telling me again about some of the mean things his old man had done to people. That's when I told Newton what I had witnessed."

Ella drank her coffee and took a couple bites of the cinnamon bun. "Oh my, this is delicious. Latisha is a good cook."

Bowman was taken aback by her reaction to what he had just told her. He waited for some sort of remark.

"Bowman, what did Newton say when you told him?" she asked.

"Newton said, 'I don't doubt that one bit. He wanted Ella all to himself.'"

Bowman turned his eyes away and looked at the floor. He knew Ella was consumed by shame, but what Newton had said rang true.

"Well, thank you, Bowman, for confirming what I have always suspected."

Ella stood and walked out, leaving Bowman chewing on his unlit cigar.

15

Preparations

Before Ella realized it, she had driven out of Sandy Creek and was turning down the white, sandy, dirt road leading to the Soul River backwater. Fishermen would launch their boats from this shallow area and follow a small canal leading out of the backwater to the main river. Large cypress trees reached toward the sky. Their knotty knee stumps poked up all around the big trees. The swamp floor was coming to life with green duckweed and arum growing in the shallows. Tightly closed lilies raised their heads above the lush green pads as they sought the sun from beneath the water's surface.

Ella found herself standing alone at the water's edge gazing into the depths of the Soul. The dark, tannin stained water melted into the deeper parts of the river as it met the sandy banks, its color reminding her of sweet tea. She looked out across the swamp in the direction of where the duck blind used to perch between two large cypress trees. High waters had washed it away many years ago. Ella was glad to see it was gone. It was a reminder of her loss, and now with Bowman's eyewitness account of that horrible morning, she could visualize her husband's death as if she were standing right next to him. She could see Jacob struggling in the water, his life running out into the darkness of the Soul River. Tears formed in her eyes. The pain deep inside hurt more than she could stand.

A pileated woodpecker hammering away on a tree deep in the swamp startled Ella back to reality. She looked around and was relieved to see that she was alone. The river swamp was quiet and still except for the sound of birds and an occasional fish breaking the water. What a beautiful place to die. She walked to her car and got the small pistol she kept in her glove compartment. As she walked back to the water's edge, all Ella could think of was the shame inside of her. Thanks to Newton, now Bowman Whitmire knew of her humiliation.

Her suicidal ideations were interrupted by the rattling sound of a truck pulling up with a boat trailer. Panic took hold. Two young men got out of the pickup. She concealed the gun in her pocket, hoping they hadn't seen it in her hand. She had been only seconds away from putting it to her head and pulling the trigger.

As she walked to her car, the young men greeted her politely. They knew who she was, but, of course, everyone in Soul County knew Ella. She responded to them with a wave, got in her car and slowly drove home.

Langford was sitting on the front porch enjoying a glass of tea and reading a book.

"Well, how was Bowman?" he asked without looking up from his book.

Ella hadn't told him she was going to see Bowman. "He was fine, except for his horrible cough. And how did you know I went to see Bowman?"

"He called to let you know you left your purse." Langford smiled.

"His son is bringing it out. He should be here any minute. Remember, we have a party for Newton tomorrow. We'll have guests."

Ella put her hand on her forehead. "Where in the world was my mind? I have never left my purse anywhere. God, I'm losing it."

Langford followed her into the house. "Also, Gaylord Willard called and wanted to know what time to bring Newton out to the house."

Ella went straight to the kitchen and pulled out a bottle of bourbon from the cabinet. "I need a drink."

"Ella, it's only noon. Isn't it a bit early for a drink?" Langford said with surprise.

Ella turned to him. "I'm seventy-eight years old. If I want to have a shot of whiskey at any time, I will. Furthermore, it's none of your business."

Langford chuckled. "Hell, Ella, I'll have one with you."

She pulled out her bottle of Jack Daniels and poured up two good shots. "We have a lot to do before the funeral home delivers Newton's body."

They threw back their drinks and washed up the glasses.

"Follow me," Ella ordered.

Ella stood in the formal living room and studied the furniture arrangement. "I think we could move the sideboard out and put the casket right over there. This is a large room with plenty of seating. The flowers and the guestbook can go by the door."

The two were able to carefully lift the sideboard and place it in the hallway.

"How many people should we expect?" asked Ella.

Langford thought for a minute. "Around 40 to

50. Not too many. Newton only wanted his closest friends."

A knock at the door drew their attention away from funeral planning. It was Junior Whitmire with Ella's purse.

"Junior, I am so sorry you had to come out here for my blunder."

Junior smiled. "No problem, Ms. Timrod. We'll see you tomorrow."

Ella went off down the hall talking to herself and disappeared into a back room.

Langford sat down on the formal sofa and stared at the empty spot where Newton's casket would be placed. The casket was a rental due to the fact Newton wanted to be cremated. Langford laid his head back, closed his eyes and thought about Newton and how they had enjoyed each other's company.

"So sorry for you, brother. I will miss you," he whispered.

Ella emerged from the back room with a dust mop. "I called Willard Funeral Home, and they're bringing Newton in about an hour."

She pushed the mop around the floor to make sure there were no dust bunnies hiding in the corners. "I told Gaylord I wanted Newton in the formal room. He's been here before, so he knows what to do."

Ella sat down next to Langford. "I can't believe we're not having a church service and a burial in the family plot. I had it all arranged until you and Angel appeared at my door."

"Sorry, Ella, but a man's last wishes should be respected." He stood up, stretched, and started for his room.

"Where are you going, Dr. Wallace?"

"Dr. Wallace is going to take a nap."

He left Ella to her own thoughts. He knew that the casket, when it arrived, would get pushed around the room until it looked just right.

When he awoke, Langford could hear faint voices coming from the front of the house, probably from the front porch. He shook off the sleep, combed his long gray hair, pulled it back in a ponytail, stepped to the bathroom, relieved himself, and washed his hands and face.

He could hear Ella laughing. He peaked out the window to see a tall, nicely dressed black man standing on the porch talking to Ella. He looked like a businessman in his dark suit, and he was driving what looked to be a Mercedes. Langford realized who it was. Newton had told him about this gentleman. He stepped out on the porch, startling the two.

Ella looked excited to see Langford. "Did our laughter wake you, Langford?"

"No. It was time to get moving." Langford reached his hand out to meet the newcomer. "Dr. Langford Wallace."

"Tobias Williams, nice to meet you Doctor Wallace," he replied with a firm handshake.

"Call me Langford," he said with a smile.

"Langford, this gentleman is the pride of Sandy Creek," Ella blurted out excitedly as she beamed with joy.

"Oh, really? So, please, tell me," Langford asked curiously.

"Tobias graduated Harvard Law and works for a large law firm in Boston. Even though Newton was a few years older than Tobias, they formed a sort of friendship when Tobias worked for Daddy."

Ella was almost giddy with excitement having a successful attorney from up north standing on her front porch.

"Excuse me, I have to check on something inside. I'll be right back." Ella disappeared into the house.

"Langford, you know why I'm here," Tobias said quietly.

"I do, Tobias, but Ella's really fragile right now, so timing is everything."

"Wilson Timrod has got to be exposed for what he did to Mary Lou Reese. And, it's quite possible there were other victims."

"Other victims?" Langford exclaimed.

"Yes, we need to talk. I have a file of young girls from around this part of the state who disappeared and were never found. Most were considered to be runaways."

Footsteps halted their discussion. Ella pushed the screen door open. "Where are you staying, Tobias?"

"I'm going to stay in town."

Ella crossed her arms. "I don't think so. We can't let the most famous person from Soul County stay in that dump. You'll stay here, and I will not take no for an answer."

Tobias looked at Langford, then back at Ella. "Well, thank you, Ms. Timrod, for such a gracious offer."

The sound of a vehicle turned their attention to the road.

"Well, Newton's home," Ella's eyes followed the black hearse coming up the driveway.

Gaylord and Bobby were together in the front seat of the hearse, and Stancil followed driving a van. They were all dressed in suits and quickly went to work preparing the area for the casket. Ella watched every move they made.

Langford and Tobias helped carry the casket up the front steps, into the house and place it on the platform. Stancil started bringing in extra chairs, and Bobby placed the flowers sent from friends.

When it was all said and done, Ella looked at Gaylord as he wiped the perspiration from his forehead. "Do you think it might look better on the other side of the room?"

A silence fell over the room. Langford spoke up. "Ella, we're not moving him. The casket is fine here. Anyway, there will be plenty of room for people to mingle."

Gaylord let out a sigh and looked thankfully at Langford.

Ella wrung her hands. "Okay, I guess this will do." She walked up to the casket, placed her hand on it and turned to everyone. "Shall we take a look at him?"

The group was silent. Gaylord stepped forward and opened the lid. They all gathered around Newton.

"Great job, Gaylord. He looks as handsome dead as he did alive," Ella said with pride.

Stancil put his hands together as if to say a prayer.

"What now?" Ella asked.

Gaylord closed the lid. "Let's keep it closed until your guests arrive tomorrow. We'll be here early to make sure Newton is presentable."

Ella turned to Tobias. "Well, let's get you settled into a room. I'll put you in Daddy's room. You'll have a private bath." She walked away.

Tobias felt his legs go numb. He thought he was going to fall. He wanted to speak up and say, "Hell no," but he knew that would be rude.

Langford couldn't believe what he had just heard and was as surprised as Tobias. The two men looked at each other in disbelief.

"Hope your bed is more comfortable than mine," Langford whispered to Tobias, grinning at him as he walked ahead.

16

Snooping

Langford heard a knock at his door. To his surprise, it was Angel. She had returned to Ella's house alone.

"Langford, I'm going to head back to Charleston on Sunday. Dr. Travis has two surgeries scheduled for next week, and he'll need me to assist him. Do you want to return with me? What are your plans?"

Langford considered the new information about Wilson Timrod that Tobias had brought to the table and decided he would stay.

"I think I'll hang around a while. I'll call the office and have Linda clear my schedule for a few weeks. I never realized this would turn into a murder investigation." Langford gave Angel a wink and motioned for her to come inside.

Angel looked confused. "Murder investigation?" she questioned.

Langford looked out the door and both ways down the hall, then closed the door behind Angel. He motioned for her to step away from the door and over to the window so no one could hear them.

"Tobias has told me he has information on Wilson Timrod that will set this town on fire." He paused and looked out the window to be sure they were alone.

Angel perked up and leaned forward. "Well, tell me."

"After Tobias graduated from Harvard and started working as a prosecutor, he had access to people who could help him look into a certain Wilson Timrod. Then he was offered big money to join a large scale law firm in Boston. He took his information, and at the new job he had some of the best private investigators at his beck and call. That's all he has told me so far. Now, I haven't had a chance to look at his information yet, but according to him, Timrod was a murdering psychopath. I hope to spend some time with Tobias going over his information after the party tomorrow."

Angel looked away, in deep thought. "Poor Newton, this place must have been a living hell when he was younger."

Langford heard footsteps in the hall. He put his finger to his lips. He and Angel stood still, hardly breathing, hoping Ella hadn't been standing outside the door.

Angel quietly peeked out the door. "She's gone," She whispered.

Langford pulled out the file of notes and letters Newton had written describing incidents he had observed regarding his father.

"This is all Newton left for me to read. Apparently he had been writing about his father's comings and goings since he was a teenager. There's only one murder in these notes, and that is concerning Ella's husband, Jacob. He did write about seeing his father take Mary Lou Reese away and assumed he may have killed her but was afraid to pry too much. If his father found out he was snooping around, I'm sure Wilson might have disposed of Newton as well. According to Tobias, it's quite possible that there were many more murders committed by Wilson Timrod."

Langford thought for a moment. "If Newton knew about any others, he would have made notes about it. I bet there are more notes hidden in his room. It would have been just like him to have left a clue. Newton liked word and fantasy games."

Langford looked at Angel. "Can you get Ella away from the house for at least an hour?"

"Right now?" Angel asked, thinking Langford had lost his mind.

"Right now, Angel," Langford confirmed.

"What about Tobias sitting on the front porch, and Newton's casket in the front room?" Angel said anxiously. "Ella won't leave y'all here alone with Newton."

"Ella thinks the world of Tobias, She most likely trusts him more than she trusts me. I think she'll go. We've got to try. I need to get into Newton's room and do some snooping without Ella around," said Langford.

Angel thought for a minute. "I know. Latisha wanted me to run to Walmart and pick up table-cloths and napkins with some sort of festive look, anything but white. I'll tell Ella I need her help, and that I'd like to spend a little more time with her."

"Okay, get to it." Langford was excited to become a sleuth instead of a doctor.

Ten minutes or so passed before Langford observed Angel and Ella driving away. He quickly ran down the stairs to where Tobias was sitting, reading a thick file.

"Tobias, I need your help. We need to get into Newton's room and snoop around a little while Ella is gone." Langford turned and hurried to the stairs. "Follow me."

"Langford, what are you looking for?" Tobias questioned.

As the two men walked up the stairs to Newton's room, Langford explained that Newton had kept notes on his father.

"Newton knew more than we thought. I'm sure of it. There must be something about the murders. He shared a lot with me after we found out we were half brothers. We were extremely close, especially in his last years."

The door to Newton's room was locked. Langford fiddled in his pocket for the key, inserted it and pushed the door open. The drapes were pulled, and the room was dim. Langford turned on several lights. The bookshelves were filled with countless books.

"Newton was an avid reader," Langford said.

Tobias wandered around the room looking over the titles. He was in awe of the collection. "I would love to purchase some of these books."

Langford laughed. "You'll have to take that up with the county library. But, since you are the pride of Soul County, I'm sure they'll work something out."

The two men scanned the room for anything

out of the ordinary. Langford had been through Newton's safe earlier in the week. They looked under the bed, behind furniture, in the closet and even felt the walls for a hidden panel. Finally, they both sat on the end of the bed.

"Well, Tobias, he was a pretty smart fellow. Maybe he didn't leave any documents other than the ones I have," said Langford.

Tobias got up and walked to the bookcase. Something had caught his eye. He stood in front of one book and studied it. The cover was pretty worn, as if it had been opened and closed a lot.

"Langford, are you familiar with these books?" Tobias pointed to a copy of *A Piece of the Fox's Hide* by Katharine Boling, and right next to it, *Final Truth: The Autobiography of a Serial Killer.* "These books are about notorious killers from around this area. The Bighams were just down right evil, and Donald "Pee Wee" Gaskins was a vicious killer.

Langford walked over and stood beside Tobias. "I'm not familiar with them, but if you're from around here, then you know about these books. What are your thoughts, Tobias?"

"Look at his collection and how well organized it is." Tobias waved his arms over the shelves. "All of the books in this section are classics, so why would

Newton stick these two books on the shelf among the great ones? That's not to say they're not interesting reads. This one has been looked at a great deal by the looks of the worn cover. Newton was a gentle soul, not one to entertain violence, even in his literature." Tobias tapped his finger on the two books.

"Well, let's see." Langford pulled out the two books and handed one to Tobias. "You take one, and I'll take one."

They sat down, Tobias in the wingback chair and Langford at the foot of the bed. As Tobias flipped through the pages of *Fox's Hide,* he noticed on page 12 that someone had underlined letters that spelled out *ASK PEE WEE.*

"It's in the book you have there, Langford. Look at this." Tobias pointed out the underlined letters.

Langford was inspecting each page and the book jacket slipped off. A note in Newton's handwriting was written on the inside of the jacket cover. They sat down together to read it.

Tobias,

Remember when we would hang out together during tobacco season? I would share my books with you. You especially loved "The Hardy Boys" mysteries. We would talk about solving crimes and word clues and had secret handshakes. Of course, if my father knew about our friendship, he would have fired you and beat me senseless. He never found out.

I knew you would help Langford figure this out. You and I have had a great friendship over many years, and I trust you to help make this right.

I have always kept your secret about Mary Lou Reese. I know you loved her. When you told me about my father pushing her into his car, and then finding out the next day that Mary Lou was dead, I knew my father had something to do with it. I know because I was watching from my bedroom window when he shoved her into the car.

As a kid I was a bit of a snoop, especially around this big old house. I found hidden places that no one knew about. After my dad had his stroke, I was able to investigate his office. I hit the jackpot there and found news articles about missing girls along with notes he had written about raping and killing Mary Lou. Apparently he saw the two of you together talking and laughing and assumed there was more to it. My father was a sick, perverse man.

In his office under his desk, you'll see a small

hole in the floor. Place a nail in it and pull up. It's all there.

Fix this wickedness, and let the people know my father was as bad as the Bighams and PEE WEE.

Newton

Tobias kept the *Final Truth: The Autobiography of a Serial Killer* and Langford put the other book back in place. Together, they headed downstairs to the old man's office.

"We must hurry. Angel and Ella will be back soon, and this might be our only chance to retrieve the papers."

The two men got on their knees by the desk. Langford found the tiny hole. He reached into his pocket for a small penknife, poked it into the hole and slowly lifted the floorboard. Sure enough, the papers were there, just as Newton had said in his note.

Langford handed the papers to Tobias.

The two men started reading Wilson Timrods little black notebooks. The old man had pretty much written everything about the murders. What he did, how he did it, it was all detailed out in black and white. They couldn't believe their eyes. The man had actually written down details. Except where he had buried the bodies. They needed bodies to back up the writings.

"Here, take these and put them in your files. We can look at them more indept after the party tomorrow. We're going to have to inform Ella that we're staying a little longer. Not sure she's going to be happy with the extended stay."

With everything back in place, the two men retreated to the porch with a bourbon in hand to celebrate their findings. It was time to come up with a plan for the coming week.

17

The Service

It was a long time ago, but the trauma from Ella's childhood remained ever-present and undeniable. Even though her father was dead, there was no place to run or hide from her thoughts of him, and there was still no escape from the flashbacks. Evil resided in the big house, and it ruled with an iron fist.

Ella lay in her bed with her hands over her face feeling the shame of those long past years. She was stuck in a world of horrible memories. They seemed to live with her on a daily basis, especially now that she was aware of certain people knowing her deep secrets. Her pain didn't draw blood or leave bruises. It was an invisible injury. The make-believe world she lived in couldn't stop the hurt deep in Ella's soul. Now as an old woman, Ella would have to face her demons. All she wanted to do was die.

She sat up and looked out her window. The sun was rising over the fields of freshly planted corn. The tender green sprouts were peeking up in perfect rows, reminding Ella of the great tobacco crop that once grew all around the house. Workers back then had been busy in the fields, but now it was a lonesome place.

She didn't look forward to this day, the day of Newton's funeral. People she had never met would invade her house and yard. Ella worried they'd steal something out of the house or mess up her flower beds. She wanted it over and prayed it would pass quickly.

Downstairs, as Ella walked by the casket in the living room, she stopped to straighten the casket spray. It was beautiful, but she noticed some of the flowers were beginning to wilt.

"Not acceptable," she said out loud.

"I'm sorry, were you talking to me?" Tobias questioned.

She turned to see Tobias sitting in the corner of the room in the shadows.

"Oh, no, Tobias, it's the flowers. Some are wilting. I must call the florist and have some fresh ones brought out."

Tobias walked over to the casket. "Let's have a look." He touched a few flowers. "Oh, I think it looks fine. Just one or two here need to be removed."

He pulled out a couple of daisies and arranged the rest a bit. "There now, that's better."

Ella eyed his fix. "Well, I guess so. Frankly, I'm already tired of this day, and I pray it gets over quickly."

"Come, Ella, let's have a cup of coffee," Tobias suggested in his slow and gentle way.

The two walked into the kitchen to the smell of fresh brewed coffee. Ella could see Langford out back sitting in one of her rusty metal chairs, eyes closed as if he were meditating. He was dressed in a pair of khakis and a denim shirt. His ponytail was neatly pulled back. She admired Langford's ability to cope with all that was going on. She wished she had the calm and peace he seemed to possess.

Ella crinkled up her face and turned to Tobias. "Why doesn't he cut his hair? He's a physician. Surely his patients find that distasteful. Is he going to wear those clothes today?" she asked.

"Ella, I think that's his business. I'm sure he doesn't feel as if he has to prove himself to anyone," Tobias said with a smile.

Langford stood and walked up the back steps into the kitchen.

"How's Newton this morning? Have you checked on him?" Langford winked and smiled at Tobias.

Ella didn't respond. She turned her back to the two and walked out of the kitchen. "I'll be on the porch reading the paper."

Ella did her best to escape into the local news. She drank her coffee and tried not to think about the day and what Newton's crazy friends would be like.

The morning seemed to drag by until a truck pulling a trailer maneuvered into the driveway. Junior Whitmire and the crew from the Barbeque Hut had arrived to set up.

Ella went inside and asked Langford to show Junior where to park his truck and trailer. She then retreated to her room to prepare for the day's event. She put on a beautiful spring dress she had ordered years ago, checked her hair and descended the stairs to the living room.

It was now 11:00 a.m. The service would be at 1:00 p.m., and Gaylord Willard had already arrived. Ella was amazed at his early arrival. He and Stancil had made sure Newton's makeup and hair looked right.

Bitty and Angel were standing in front of the casket. Angel had her arm around her mother. Bitty couldn't believe her eyes seeing Newton all dressed up in a suit. She really didn't remember much about the morning she and Ella had gone to the funeral home. It was one big blur.

Ella walked up to Bitty and hugged her. "So comforting to see my good friend here to support me during this sad time."

Tobias and Langford entered the room, and Ella introduced Tobias to Angel.

Angel smiled. "A pleasure to meet the pride of Soul County, Mr. Williams."

"Please, call me Tobias."

Langford interrupted, "Ella, do you have a minute? Tobias and I would like a word."

"Certainly, we can go to Daddy's office." Ella led the way.

Langford hesitated a minute. "Ella, I feel really bad having to ask you this, but Tobias and I would like to be here for the scattering of the ashes. Gaylord said he would have them ready by the end of this coming week. We could plan to do it next weekend. Would you mind if we stayed a while longer with you?"

Ella thought for a moment. She turned and looked out the window. "Well, I really want to get all of this over with. Since Newton's wishes were to be cremated and scattered in the Soul River, then we shall do it. You and Tobias are welcome to stay a little longer, but please don't stay too much longer. I'm not used to people around the house."

Ella abruptly turned to go. Holding on to the doorknob, she motioned for them to get out of the office. "I don't want strangers snooping around," She locked the door after them.

Langford and Tobias took note of Ella locking the door and were glad they'd been able to get the letters and documents from the hiding place under the desk.

The band arrived and set up on the back porch. It was perfect. Junior had his men erect a large tent, while he and Latisha were busy getting the food together. Junior had stayed up most of the night roasting the pig. Bowman was in charge of the bar. He sat in a lawn chair while one of his bartenders served up alcoholic beverages.

Bitty found Langford and voiced her concern that Ella had disappeared and guests were arriving.

He searched all over and peered around the open door to her bedroom. Ella was looking out the window at the menagerie of people. She saw men holding hands and a couple of guys dressed in women's clothing, greeting each other with kisses on the cheek. Ella wasn't sure if one or two of them were men or women. She was shocked and didn't know how to greet them. The only normal people there, in Ella's eyes, were Sonia and Jay Sumpter, the Gaylords and, of course, Bitty, Angel, Langford and Tobias.

"Ella, guests are arriving. What are you doing in your room?" Langford asked, interrupting her thoughts.

She shook her head. "How in the world can I mix with these kinds of people? I don't even know what to say to them."

Langford laughed. "Ella, you don't have to say anything, Introduce yourself, and they will do the rest. Be nice, Ella. They won't bite."

Langford escorted Ella downstairs and broke the ice by introducing her to Tom Bailey and Billy Rhea. They were very talkative and extremely effeminate. They went on and on about Newton and how long they had been friends. She smiled and continued on to the next guest, Loraine Miles, a drag queen. She was in full regalia. She touched Ella's arm. "Oh honey, Newton just loved this outfit when I was on stage." She smiled and gave Ella a big hug. Ella's head was spinning.

Finally, Gaylord called everyone into the living room. Langford moved to the front of the packed room and spoke about Newton. He looked at Ella, she shook her head. She wasn't about to get up and say anything in front of this crowd. After several of Newton's friends had their say, everyone streamed by the casket and said goodbye. Gaylord closed the lid. Slowly, the crowd left the room and joined the party in the backyard.

Ella leaned close to Bitty. "I can't believe not even a prayer was said over him."

Bitty squeezed Ella's hand. "Well, we can if we want to. We'll just do it in private."

Ella and Bitty walked up to the casket, placed their hands on it, and Bitty spoke the most beautiful prayer Ella had ever heard.

"Thank you, Bitty." A tear slipped down Ella's cheek.

The two joined the group outside and found a shady spot. Bitty sat next to Ella to comfort her, and the rest danced and drank. Ella couldn't believe her eyes. Men danced together, and women were holding hands. She was the only one not having fun. Her head hurt from the music.

Finally, Jay Sumpter approached Ella. "Ms. Timrod, could I have a word with you?" he asked politely.

"Of course, Jay, but can we go somewhere quiet? This music's too loud for my old ears," she replied.

They walked out toward the big barn where her father had kept his car and truck.

"First of all, thank you for giving the land back." Jay's voice quivered.

"That was all Newton. It was his land to give," Ella said.

"Would you mind if we went ahead and did some planting? I know probate will take at least a year. Sonia and I have plans for a new business for her and Jay Jr. They want to start a vegetable stand in Riverton," Jay said proudly.

Ella was surprised to hear this. "Well, I think that's wonderful. I love my garden. It gives me so much pleasure. Yes, of course, please go ahead and good luck."

Jay thanked her and walked back to join his wife and son at the party.

Langford and Tobias watched Ella open the barn door and walk inside.

"Let's see what she's up to," said Langford.

The two men quietly approached the barn, stopping just close enough to be able to peer inside. They could see Ella, looking at a dusty old Cadillac in mint condition.

"That's the same car Wilson Timrod drove Mary Lou Reese away in. I wonder if there could be any evidence left from long ago?" whispered Tobias with a grimace.

Langford pushed the door open and stepped into the barn, surprising Ella. "Wow, what a nice old Cadillac. Is it yours?"

Ella looked annoyed that they had imposed on her moment alone. "No, it was my Daddy's."

Tobias walked slowly around the car trying to get a good look inside. The windows were dusty, concealing any signs there might be of Mary Lou Reese ever having been in the car. He figured Wilson Timrod was probably too smart to leave any evidence.

"Ella, I believe this is the car your father had when I worked for him during my senior year in high school," said Tobias.

"Most likely. I believe it was a year later he had the stroke and was bedridden," Ella said sadly.

"It sure is a well kept car. Not a scratch on it," Langford said, stepping closer.

Ella ran her hand across the roof, picking up dust. "He always kept cars for a long time, and he took good care of them. This was his last car. I need to have it washed and then covered."

Tobias spoke up. "Ella, I know a couple of young men in Sandy Creek who detail cars. How about I drive it over in the morning? Will it start?"

Ella thought for a minute. "How much would something like that cost?."

"About fifty dollars to detail it. I'll tell you what. I'll pay," Tobias offered, looking at Langford.

"Oh, no. I'll pay," said Ella.

"Okay, Ella, whatever suits you," Tobias said politely.

Ella seemed satisfied with having this done. "You'll drive carefully, and take Langford with you. I need some time alone."

The sound of Angel calling interrupted the conversation. Langford motioned for them to go.

"I think the party is coming to an end. We best go and say our goodbyes."

Tobias glanced at Langford; they were thinking the same thought. He pulled the barn door closed, and they all headed back to the guests.

As the day was ending, the last of the guests drove away. Gaylord and his sons loaded Newton back into the hearse. His next stop was the crematorium in Columbia. The barbeque folks had cleaned up and pulled away. The band left a little early for a gig at the Barbeque Hut later in the evening.

Bitty and Angel gave Ella a big hug.

Angel pulled Langford aside. "I'll be back next weekend," she said to him.

Langford stepped closer to her. "Wish us luck."

18

The Cadillac

Ella shouted her orders at the two men as they slowly backed the car out of the garage. "Y'all be careful now, you hear? That car is special to me."

Langford and Tobias nodded and slowly drove away.

"So, what's the plan, Tobias?" Langford asked curiously.

Tobias smiled at Langford. They headed toward the Soul River bridge. "Are we something or what?" Tobias laughed. He leaned back into the driver's seat draping his arm over the steering wheel of the old Cadillac.

"A black attorney who hasn't lived in the south for decades and a white-haired, old hippie doctor from Charleston. Folks are going to think we're drug dealers, especially seeing us driving around in an antique Cadillac."

The two broke out in laughter.

"Here's the plan, Langford. We'll take the car to my Dad's house in Sandy Creek, go over it with a fine-tooth comb and see what we can see. Then wash it and head back."

Tobias waited for an acknowledgement from Langford.

"Okay, that sounds like a plan. Are your parents still alive?" Langford asked.

"My mother died a few years ago, and my dad, who is ninety-two, is in a nursing home. They left the house to me before Momma died. She knew Daddy was quickly losing what mind he had left. Daddy doesn't even know who I am when I visit. Been renting the old house to a couple, but they moved away. It's empty now. I have a man who keeps the yard up. I'm seriously thinking of putting it on the market."

"Sorry to hear about your dad," Langford said sadly.

Tobias looked out over the farmland. "My life is different now, and I don't have an ounce of desire to return to Soul County. I needed to get as far away as I could from the memories of sweating in a tobacco barn. One thing I want to do before I cut my ties with Sandy Creek and Soul County is to prove Wilson Timrod was a murdering lunatic."

Tobias slammed his hand on the steering wheel.

They crossed the Soul River and turned onto Sandy Creek Road. The Cadillac floated along as if it were flying above the pavement. Langford looked out at the beautiful black water cutting its way through the dense swamp. The scene was surreal. It was warm, and every plant was a brilliant green.

"Man, what a ride." Langford rolled his window down and let the warm breeze flow over him.

His gray ponytail flipped around in the wind. It brought back memories of his college days and of running with the crazy youth movement of long ago. Civil rights, Vietnam, crazy times.

"We're going to expose Wilson Timrod for what he really was." Tobias, glanced at Langford with a look of pure determination.

"We'll do our best," Langford gave Tobias a pat on the shoulder.

As they approached Sandy Creek, Tobias turned down a dirt road before they actually got into the small community. Langford could see a house with a barn in the back surrounded by live oak trees and a few large pines.

Tobias pulled around behind the house. "I don't think anyone will bother us." He looked across the fields toward Sandy Creek.

Tobias could hear the Sunday morning choir at the AME Methodist Church, singing with the swaying rhythm he remembered from his youth. He would spend almost the entire day in church listening to Reverend Manigo pound on the pulpit, pacing back and forth and flipping through his Bible reciting verse after verse. Tobias couldn't help but laugh at how the Reverend would get all caught up in the preaching and, before Tobias knew it, it was mid afternoon.

"Let's do this," said Tobias, shaking off the memory.

The two went to work on the Cadillac, starting up front. So far, the car seemed to be clean, with not a single clue. Langford moved to the back seat, laid down as best he could and looked under the front seat. Using his penlight to look in the dark recesses, he noticed a piece of paper was caught up under the seat. He reached in and pulled out a part of what appeared to be a check. It was fragile and a bit faded, but he could make out the name *Reese*.

"Tobias, I've found something," Langford said excitedly.

Tobias jerked open the back door and slid

into the back seat next to Langford. Langford gently handed him the piece of the check.

"This is great. Something with Mary Lou's name on it. But we need more, like blood stains, or a piece of her clothing," said Tobias.

Langford frowned. "Are you sure?"

"Listen, I've spent my career sending criminals to jail and keeping some out of jail. I know how evidence works and what a defense attorney can do, especially a good one, and I am a good one," said Tobias.

"But this will never go to trial. Wilson Timrod is dead. All we want to do is expose him for what he did," Langford said.

"True, Langford, but what if Ella gets upset about her good family name getting trashed and decides to sue me?" asked Tobias.

"I won't let her do that, Tobias," Langford said reassuringly.

"I hope not, because my law firm would eat her alive, and I truly don't want that to happen," he said sternly.

Langford sensed Tobias's profound anger for Wilson Timrod. He took a deep breath and half-heartedly wished he had returned to Charleston with Angel.

Finally, they opened the trunk. There were assorted tools for changing a flat, a couple of oily rags and a small, red toolbox from Sears. Tobias opened it. Inside he found a knife, typically used by a fisherman to filet fish.

"Wonder what he used this for?" Tobias carefully examined the knife.

After they inspected the car and found nothing else, they drove over to the automatic car wash in Riverton and let the machines do the hard work.

"I thought we were going to actually hand-wash this car," Langford said as they watched the brushes swish over the black Cadillac.

Tobias laughed. "Ella won't know the difference."

Langford didn't say much on the way back to Ella's house. He was deep in thought about how driven Tobias was to prove that Wilson Timrod murdered Mary Lou Reese. "Tobias, tell me about you and Mary Lou, if you don't mind?"

The car came to a sudden stop. Langford was caught off guard. "Tobias, what in the world are you doing? Trying to kill us?"

"Listen, Langford, nothing ever happened between us. It was a simple friendship. Mary Lou and I were close in conversation only. We would spend hours talking about all sorts of things. She was nothing but poor white trash to most, but she was an angel to me. I loved her, but I knew nothing could ever come of us together. If I touched a white girl, I knew I would pay, not only from some redneck white boys, but my Daddy would not be happy. She deserved better than being raped and beaten and left to die on the edge of the river swamp. That son of a bitch, Wilson Timrod, killed Mary Lou, and I watched him drive her away to her death in this very car."

"I see this has been eating away at you, Tobias. Why didn't you ever tell someone?"

Tobias put his hand to his mouth. A tear appeared in the corner of his eye and slowly slid down his cheek. "That's just it, Langford, I did tell someone."

"Who?" Langford said with surprise.

"My grandfather, Chainy." More tears appeared.

Langford reached over and placed his hand on Tobias's shoulder, giving him a reassuring grip. "It's okay, Tobias. What did your grandfather say?"

"He told me to mind my own business and stay out of white folks' comings and goings. He said it would most likely get me in trouble. He sent me home and told me not to come back to work at the barn. That it was school time, and I needed to study."

Tobias shook his head. "I've never forgiven him for turning his back."

Now Tobias was sobbing. Langford reached in his pocket for his handkerchief and handed it to him.

"Sometimes, Tobias, a good cry can help cleanse one's soul. Let's get this road yacht back to Ella. Are you okay to drive?" asked Langford.

Tobias nodded.

Ella was delighted with the car. She watched Tobias back the Cadillac into the dusty barn.

"I should buy a car cover, or maybe I'll just sell it."

Tobias crossed his arms and thought for a moment. "Ella, how much are you asking?"

Ella was admiring the cleaning job. She opened the driver's door, sat down and placed her hands on the steering wheel. She appeared to be deep in thought and in another place.

Langford turned and looked at Tobias as if he had lost his mind. "Are you serious?" Langford asked quietly so Ella wouldn't hear.

Tobias spoke out the side of his mouth. "Sure am."

"Find out how much it's worth, and we'll work on a final number," Ella got out of the car, closed the door and walked back to the house.

The two followed her. Langford, walking close to Tobias, looked at him inquiringly, wondering why Tobias would want the car and what he was going to do with it.

Ella prepared a wonderful Sunday lunch and set a formal table in the dining room.

"I don't get to do this often. Actually, I can't remember the last time I set this table for more than one. Newton wouldn't join me. I set him a place many times, but he never presented himself. He would slip down the back steps, make a plate of food and disappear into his world of secrecy. So, I stopped using this room. Bitty and I always sat in the kitchen to eat when she came over."

Ella took a deep breath. "Since I have guests, I want to sit down to Sunday dinner with my fine china and flatware. I'm tired of eating in the kitchen."

"You've five places set. Who else is coming?" Langford asked.

Ella smiled. "Bitty and Stanley. They should

be arriving soon. They wanted to see Angel off. I invited Angel as well, but she had to get back to Charleston."

"Well, this is truly special, Ella. Thank you," Tobias said sincerely.

The back door slammed. "Anybody home?" Bitty shouted from the kitchen. "Potato salad and green beans just as you ordered, Ella."

Bitty and Stanley entered with big smiles. They seemed so happy now that Angel had come back into their lives.

Ella put the fried chicken and squash casserole on the sideboard alongside a few other yummy looking dishes. Langford filled the tea glasses, and the group settled into a wonderful Sunday dinner.

Later in the afternoon, Langford retired to his room for a nap. Tobias took a stroll down memory lane over at the old tobacco barns. Bitty and Stanley said their goodbyes and headed home.

The house fell silent. The lingering smell of food still wafted through the kitchen as Ella washed the last dish, dried it and put it back in the china cabinet. She insisted on doing dishes, she didn't want anyone breaking a single piece of her fine china.

She could see Tobias across the road wandering around the barns. She had an uneasy feeling that he was up to something but couldn't put her finger on it. She squeezed a little lotion on her hands and continued to keep an eye on him as she rubbed the lotion into her old, dry skin.

Ella noticed Tobias looking up into the rafters as he stood in the doorway of one of the barns. Then he sat down on a box by the entrance for a while just staring at the ground, head in hands. Ella could tell Tobias was reminiscing. She worried he might even know too much about her own horrible secrets.

How could Tobias know unless Newton or maybe even Langford told him? Was it possible that everybody knew what kind of man my father really was?

It would ruin the Timrod name, and Ella couldn't live with such shame. The pistol in her glove compartment came to mind as did the bottle of valium in her dresser drawer.

Footsteps in the hallway alerted Ella to Langford's entrance. "Great nap. Where's Tobias?" Langford asked.

"He's across the road rummaging through the old barns," Ella replied, abandoning her dark thoughts.

Langford filled a glass with water and drank it down. "I think I'll join him. Care to come with me?"

"I'm tired. I think I'll go to my room and relax for a while," she said wearily.

"Of course. See you for cocktails," Langford gave her a wink and smiled.

"Sure." Ella turned and walked down the hall. She ascended the stairs slowly, thinking how she had enjoyed the dinner but was worn out from cooking and company.

Langford strolled across the road to where Tobias was reflecting on the day that Mary Lou Reese rode away with Wilson Timrod to her death.

"Langford, I've read the newspaper articles we dug out of the floor of the old man's office. Wilson Timrod seemed to enjoy saving news articles about missing girls. I also re-read his notes from the murders. I found a handwritten note about Mary Lou. It was pretty bad, lots of hate in his thinking. He wrote how angry he was that a white girl would even talk to a black boy. Of course, he used a different descriptive word.

"My thought is that we can't really prove he was involved in some of the other deaths around this part of the state," Tobias said with a look of resignation. "But, we can work on proving he killed Mary Lou Reese, because we have a witness to him driving her away."

The prosecutor was coming out in Tobias. He was ready to do what needed to be done, and that was to tell Ella about the day he, himself, saw her father push Mary Lou into the Cadillac and drive away. He would show her the articles and the note.

Ella watched the two men from her bedroom window. She knew something was surely up. From what she could see, they appeared to be immersed in a very serious conversation.

She lay down on her bed and fell into a deep sleep but was shaken awake by one of her nightmares involving her father. These dreams often haunted Ella's sleep. Many times she would get up and wander the halls and rooms looking for answers.

She sat up. The clock downstairs chimed 5:00 p.m. "Well, I better get up and check on my guests," Ella said under her breath.

She found Tobias and Langford sitting on the back porch having an evening cocktail.

"I see you started without me," Ella said.

"Oh sorry, Ella, we just sat down. We figured

you were tired and needed rest," Langford pulled a chair up for her.

"Have a seat. I'll make you a drink. Same as usual?"

"Yes, same. I don't venture too far away from my norm," she said with resolve.

Ella sipped her bourbon, placed it on the table and cleared her throat. "Bitty's coming over in the morning to help me with a few things."

She hesitated, then added, "I've decided to go through all of Newton's books before they go to the library. I want to make sure there are no handwritten notes in them. The library is in dire need of good books and could sell some of the first editions to raise funds."

"Ella, going through them is a great idea. Who knows what secrets could be hidden in his books?" Tobias agreed.

Langford nodded in agreement.

"In the morning, go to Newton's room and have your pick of a couple books for your own libraries. Then, please find somewhere to go or something to do outside the house, because Bitty and I will be cleaning and going through the books together."

"Thank you, Ella. We can do that. I'm sure we can find some trouble in town. Maybe we'll go to Sandy Creek and have lunch at the Barbeque Hut," replied Langford, looking at Tobias.

They both knew very well what they would be up to tomorrow, digging around and looking for information.

19

The Note

Ella was sleeping soundly until a dream took her back to the dark days of her childhood. The presence of something sinister stood over her as she tossed and turned in her sleep.

In her nightmare, she looks up at the form of a man, face covered with a black cloth mask. The man is tall and looms over her for a while. She is frightened and turns her head away. She feels the cover removed from her body and hands touching her in places that make her uncomfortable. She freezes, and in her mind she knows it's her father. Eyes closed tightly, she goes away to a better place.

Ella jerked awake sweating and breathing hard. She sat up and put her feet on the floor. Her chest tightened, and panic gripped her body. The clock read 3:00 a.m. Softly crying, she rocked back and forth on the edge of the bed.

"Oh, please, how do I stop this madness?"

she said sadly.

She opened her bedside table and picked up the bottle of valium. It was full. Ella thought if she took the whole bottle all her pain would be gone. She lay back down, buried her head in her pillow and cried like a baby. She finally fell back to sleep with the full bottle of valium still clutched in her hand.

Sunbeams traveled up her bed and slowly illuminated Ella's face. She struggled to open her eyes, which were filled with crusty, dried tears.

Oh, my, I know I look a mess. She got up and managed to make her way to the bathroom. She wet a washcloth and wiped the night's misery from her face, brushed her hair and donned her robe and slippers. Silently, she made her way to the kitchen, hoping to be the only one up. As she rounded the corner, she could see through the window that Langford was meditating out in the yard.

"Oh, God, I can't wait till when the company will be gone, and I can get back to normal," she said crossly.

With coffee in hand, she headed to the front porch to be alone, only to find Tobias already taking up a chair.

He stood and greeted her. "Good morning, Ella, I hope you slept well."

"Not really. I didn't have a good night, and I apologize if I seem grumpy. I want to have my coffee in silence if you don't mind," she said rudely.

"Sorry to hear. I'll leave you to yourself and join Langford in the backyard."

Tobias picked up his coffee and left Ella alone.

"Thank you," she said.

Tobias walked down the hall to find Langford and to plan their day. With meditation over, Langford joined Tobias in the kitchen. Both men just stared at each other.

Finally, Langford said, "Tobias, I've been thinking about all this mess, and I want to run something by you."

Tobias sat down. "Start running."

Langford peered over Tobias's shoulder to make sure Ella was not within earshot of their conversation. He looked down the hall and could see her still sitting on the porch. Langford pulled up a chair and leaned forward toward Tobias so only Tobias could hear what he had to say.

"Look, we both know Wilson Timrod killed

Mary Lou Reese. But these other missing girls? It would take us forever to find anything out about them. Let's make Mary Lou's murder solid. We have you and the notebooks we found from the hidden place."

"Let's take a ride. I'd feel more comfortable speaking outside of this house." Tobias stood up.

Langford nodded in agreement. "You driving, or do we take the Caddy?"

"I'll drive my car," Tobias said.

Langford stuck his head out the front door. "Good morning, Ella."

Ella gazed at Langford without emotion. "I'll tell you, as well. I want to be left alone for a while before Bitty gets here."

"Of course. I was coming to tell you we're off to check out town and have lunch at the Barbeque Hut. See you later today," Langford said with a smile.

"Good. Enjoy your sightseeing. Not much to see in Riverton, just closed up shops and deserted tobacco warehouses," Ella mumbled. She turned away from him and continued to read her paper.

Tobias's black Mercedez pulled out of the driveway, and together they headed toward Riverton.

At last, Ella was alone in the house. She needed to take care of a few important issues before Bitty arrived. Standing in front of her father's office, she put the key in the door and pushed it open. In his desk drawer, she found a skinny piece of doweling. Bending down under the old desk, Ella placed the doweling in the small hole and pulled up. The secret compartment opened. She almost hit her head on the desk above when she saw that the compartment was empty.

"What in God's name?" Struggling, Ella stood up.

"Where are the notebooks and news articles?" Her words seem to echo through the house.

She walked back and forth trying to remember if Newton had a key to the office. *Oh, but the door had been unlocked for a while. I locked it myself the other day, the day of the funeral. Newton had to have taken the papers before he killed himself.*

Ella rushed up the stairs to Newton's room and unlocked the door. The room was dark and cool. She pushed back the drapes to let the light in and turned on a few lights.

Where to begin looking? She began to panic. *Okay, stop. Go get dressed, and pull yourself together.*

Ella turned and left the room. She heard someone

at the back door.

"Ella, I'm here," Bitty called out to her.

Ella shouted down the stairs. "I'll be down in a few minutes. Getting dressed."

Bitty made herself a cup of coffee and sat at the table waiting for Ella.

Ella appeared, dressed in her work clothes. "Good morning, Bitty."

"Morning."

Bitty looked at Ella's face and could tell she'd had a bad night. She had seen this many times and felt sorry for her friend. Bitty knew Ella had nightmares, and she also knew why, but she kept quiet about it. Bitty dared not mention it to Ella, because they would only have words. She didn't want to start the day with negative notions. If Ella brought it up, then Bitty would discuss it.

Bitty, as well, had her own run-in with Wilson Timrod. She thought about the time when she was sixteen. Ella was away. He came down to the kitchen and trapped her in the pantry and tried to assault her. Newton was just a boy and came running into the room looking for his dad. This saved her from the same fate that haunted Ella. Wilson Timrod never tried again with Bitty. She kept her eyes open and did her best to stay away from him.

"Well, are you ready to go through all those books?" Ella asked.

"Yep, I sure am. Stanley left these boxes he got from the Piggly Wiggly. I'll get a few to take up with us."

Ella looked out the back door at the stack of cardboard boxes. "I think this should be plenty. Please thank Stanley for me."

Once in Newton's room, Ella thought of a plan to go through every book herself. She took notice of the empty spots where Tobias and Langford had taken a few books for themselves.

"Bitty, I'll pull the book, look through it and hand it to you to place in a box."

Bitty looked at Ella a bit confused. "This would go faster if we both pull books. Don't you agree?"

"That does make sense, but I need to be sure Newton didn't leave any personal letters or hand-written notes in any of these books."

She held a book to her chest and smiled at Bitty.

Bitty knew Ella, and she knew she was up to something. "Okay, we'll do it your way," agreed Bitty.

Before long, they were down to the last of the books and had found nothing.

Ella got a notebook out to write down the titles. Bitty called them out while Ella cataloged each one.

Ella kept thinking about the books the two men had taken. She would have to go into their rooms and check those as well.

"I'll be right back. I need to get the names of the ones Langford and Tobias took," Ella said.

Bitty sat down to rest while Ella disappeared down the hall.

Ella went to Langford's room first, found the books and leafed through them, but there was nothing.

She went to her Daddy's room where Tobias was staying. Lying on the bedside table was *Final Truth: The Autobiography of a Serial Killer*. As she picked the book up, the cover came loose, revealing the handwritten message. Ella gasped as she read what Newton had written. Now she knew who had the papers from her Daddy's desk.

Ella calmly walked back to find Bitty lying down on Newton's bed.

"This is a comfortable mattress, Ella," Bitty said with a relaxed mumble.

Ella needed to get rid of Bitty. She started thinking up a good lie. "Bitty, I think I'm done with the books. We'll leave them, and I'll get the library to send someone over to haul them off. We're not lugging these heavy boxes downstairs. One of us could fall."

"Smart thinking, Ella. We are both too old to do a man's work," Bitty agreed.

Ella plopped down on the end of the bed.

"I'm beat. I had a bad night and didn't sleep much. Would you mind if we call it a day? I'm thinking of taking a long nap," Ella yawned.

Bitty sat down next to her. "Bad dreams again, Ella?"

Ella nodded. "Yes, been up and down all night."

"I understand, my friend," Bitty empathized.

Bitty picked up Newton's phone and called Stanley to come pick her up.

"Come on, let's go downstairs. It won't take Stanley long to get here."

Ella sat down on the back porch thinking about everything that had transpired over the last week. She now knew that Langford and Tobias had found the papers her father had saved about the murders. She started to cry and thought again about the bottle of pills and the gun in her car. *You old bat. You're too vain to kill yourself. Why don't you just face it all?*

She walked around her yard and studied her flowers. The vegetable garden had sprouted. Beans, cucumbers and yellow squash had popped up.

All around her were memories. Ella found herself standing in the barn at the water spigot, the same spot Mary Lou Reese was seen before getting in the car.

"My Daddy killed that poor girl," she whispered.

Ella now had evidence he had also killed Jacob, her beloved husband. She really had no reason not to believe Bowman, who had actually witnessed the murder.

Her abuser was also a murderer. She shook her head in disgust.

She walked over to the old tobacco barns thinking deeply about this entangled mess, but despite everything, what still profoundly troubled her was the lasting damage to the Timrod name if all this got out.

Right now, all Ella wanted to do was escape. She walked back to the house, went to her room and fell into a deep sleep.

20

Old Friends

The Mercedes sped along the blacktop toward Riverton. Langford and Tobias were deep in conversation and failed to see the county police car hidden behind a stand of pine trees. Tobias looked in his rearview mirror to see blue lights coming up behind him.

"Oh my, I think we're being pulled over by Mr. Law," Tobias said with concern.

"Glad you're driving and not me," Langford replied with a smirk.

Tobias pulled over and turned the engine off. He reached in the glove box for the registration and fished for his driver's license from his wallet.

Captain Billy Miles approached the car. He had already called the tag in, and when he heard the name on the registration, he knew he had to pull the car over.

Tobias rolled his window down. "Good day, Officer," he said respectfully.

Tobias looked up and recognized Billy. He'd been with the sheriff's department for years. He was getting older. Tobias figured he would be retired by now.

"Well, shut my mouth. This can't be for real. Tobias Williams," Billy bent over, took off his sunglasses, and smiled.

Tobias immediately jumped out of the car, grabbed the big cop and hugged him.

Langford watched the two standing in the middle of the road acting like kids.

"Langford, get out and meet Billy Miles," Tobias said gleefully.

Langford pulled himself out of the car, walked around and shook the big man's hand. Billy was around six foot four inches, had a bit of a gut and hands that could rap completely around a man's neck.

"Nice to meet you, Langford," Billy's voice was deep with a thick southern drawl.

"Likewise, Officer Miles."

"It's Billy." he winked and leaned against the car.

"I heard a rumor you were in town, Tobias. When I saw a black Mercedes coming from the direction of the Timrod place, I figured it was you."

"Yeah, I came for Newton's memorial," Tobias looked down.

"You know, a lot of folks in Riverton were upset. The memorial was by invitation only?" Billy questioned.

Langford said, "I'm sure, but that's what Newton wanted, and you know a man's last wishes should be respected."

"Oh, of course. I get that, but some didn't," Billy said.

"So, we should talk before I leave. Cover the old days and catch up," Tobias said seriously.

"I'd love to. Oh, by the way, one more month and this cop is hanging up the badge," Billy smiled.

"Staying here or moving to the beach?" Tobias asked.

"Now, what do you think? I promised Martha a place near the water, so I bought a little house on the inlet twenty years ago. You most likely will find me there a lot after next month," Billy nodded with a proud smile.

"Great. I wish you happiness." Tobias had a tearful twinkle in his eye.

"Thank you, Tobias." Billy looked away.

Langford picked up on the emotion between the two. He walked back around to the passenger side and got in the car.

Billy dug around in his shirt pocket for his card. "Here, call me when you get some time before you leave. Let's sit down and drink a beer. Bring Langford along. He might enjoy hearing some truth about you."

The men laughed.

Tobias looked at the card. "Captain Billy Miles, Soul County Sheriff's Department. How many officers work at the department now?"

"Twenty-one. That includes jailers, dispatchers, and the like. We've come a long way. After Dub dropped dead on the courthouse steps, we got a new sheriff, and he got things moving."

Billy shook Tobias's hand and waved to Langford. "Call me." Billy returned to his patrol car.

Tobias and Langford drove on to Riverton and kept going right through town.

"Where are we going?" Langford inquired.

"You'll see," Tobias smiled.

The sandy road to the mineral springs meandered through a pine and scrub oak forest. The sweet smell of yellow jasmine filled the air as the car slowly picked its way along. Suddenly, the road turned down to a beautiful clear water pond with a sandy white bottom.

Tobias stopped and got out. Langford followed.

"Oh my, Tobias, this is beautiful."

Tobias walked to the edge of the pond. He seemed far away in his thoughts, and Langford knew this place meant something special to Tobias.

"So, why did you bring me here?" Langford asked.

"Well, it's a long story, but I'll make it short." He picked up a pebble, and tossed it in the water. Little fish scurried to see what had ventured into their world.

Tobias began. "My last summer working for the Timrods, a couple of us boys would come back here and swim. One day, I decided to come alone. I needed to be by myself. It was right after Mary Lou was murdered, the end of the summer season but still hot, hotter than the lower step of Hell.

"I was swimming alone, and a truckload of white kids drove up to swim. Billy Miles was one. Billy was pretty much a quiet boy. He was strong, too, a lineman on the football team. Schools had just integrated, and I knew my senior year would be hard going. When the other boys saw me, they jumped in and tried to beat me up and hold me under the water. Next thing I knew, I saw nothing but arms and legs flailing away in the air. Billy took those guys and tossed them like rag dolls. He pulled me up and helped me to the shore. The others jumped in the truck and drove away, flipping us the bird and calling us names."

Langford started to put it all together. They must have become special friends in high school, and when Tobias went away to college, Langford guessed Billy didn't.

"So what happened next?" asked Langford.

"The two of us walked all the way to Billy's house, and his daddy gave me a ride home."

Tobias smiled, remembering their kindness.

"We were friends the entire school year. College football coaches were talking to Billy's dad, but halfway through football season Billy blew his knee out, and that was the end of it for Billy."

"How unfortunate for him. That happens a lot to high school players," Langford added.

"So, this is where I met the best friend I ever

had, well at least one of them." Tobias smiled at Langford. "Billy and I lost touch after high school. Went in different directions."

"Not to change the subject, but I need to finish my thoughts from earlier," Langford interrupted Tobias.

"I'm curious as to what's on your mind, Langford." Tobias shot him a questioning look.

"Well, as I said, we can only prove he murdered Mary Lou. Again, Wilson Timrod is dead. What good will it do to destroy his name? You know what they say about vengeance. You may as well dig two graves. So much time has passed. Ella may seem like a strong woman at times, but she is on the cusp of breaking down," Langford pled his case.

"I understand your feelings, Langford, but he was an evil man. The good people of Soul County need to know he was a murderer." Tobias clenched his fists. "He raped Mary Lou and beat her to death, leaving her body in the swamp to rot."

It suddenly dawned on Langford that there was more to Tobias and Mary Lou. "What are you not telling me, Tobias?"

Langford waited for an answer.

Tobias broke down in tears. After a minute, he got control of his emotions. "That summer, my last summer working tobacco, Mary Lou would pick me up after dark. I would sneak out and meet her down the road from Sandy Creek. She would drive her mother's old car, and we would come out here and swim. She was so beautiful with her blond hair and green eyes. When the moon was full, Mary Lou almost glowed in the light. One night we were swimming, laughing and I got a bit too close. I couldn't help myself. I kissed her. We were both caught off guard. She smiled and said it was alright."

Tobias wiped away the tears. "I swear that was all. We would laugh and talk. She and I were close but not in a sexual way, there were times I wanted more. I wanted her more than life, but I knew better. She was my friend, just like Billy."

Langford paced back and forth, thinking. "Did Billy know about your friendship?" he asked.

"He did. And he kept it a secret forever."

"How did he know?" Langford questioned.

"He walked up on us swimming one night. He didn't say a word. He turned and left. He never brought it up during our friendship."

Tobias looked out into the thick woods. "Let's

go."

Langford grabbed Tobias by the arm. "What do you say, we let it go and let Ella have her life. Telling her all about her father won't bring Mary Lou Reese back."

"Let's go. I'll think about it," Tobias pulled away from Langford.

The two men drove in silence for a while. Langford could see the tension in Tobias by the way he gripped the steering wheel.

Finally, Tobias said, "Look, Langford, I mean Ella no harm. She is a kind lady, and I truly don't want to hurt her. Let's see how the rest of the week unfolds. I may have a change of heart."

"Thank you, Tobias. That's all I ask."

Langford crossed his arms and smiled. "Hey, how about we stop in Sandy Creek at the Barbeque Hut for lunch?"

Tobias agreed. "Perfect, but first I need to make a call."

Tobias pulled over, took the card out of his pocket, and dialed Billy.

"Hey, how about a beer when you get off tomorrow? Great, yeah, I'll bring him. The River Room, yeah. We'll find it. 4:00 p.m. Got it. See you then."

The Barbeque Hut's parking lot was empty. A *Closed* sign on the door read *Death in the family.*

"I have a terrible feeling that Bowman might have died." The two men looked at each other.

Latisha came to the door and opened it. She had tears in her eyes. "Y'all come in. It's okay."

She locked the door behind them, poured them some tea, and sat at the counter. "I found him this morning on the floor in the bar. He hadn't been dead long. I called 911, but it was too late."

She cried a little, composed herself and continued. "Dr. Wallace, you need to call Angel and tell her. She would want to know for sure. We haven't really put the word out, but you know how talk spreads."

"Yes, I do. I am so sorry." Langford patted her hand.

"Latisha, you remember Tobias from Newton's memorial?"

"I do. Nice to see you again. I've heard a lot about you and all your success."

"Thank you, ma'am."

Langford stood up. "Can we do anything to help?" he asked.

Thank you, but Sandy Creek got this." Latisha smiled gratefully.

"Then we'll leave you to your quiet. I'll call Angel," said Langford.

The two men drove toward Ella's house with many thoughts in their minds. What would the next few days bring?

21

Confession

The sound of Langford talking woke Ella from her deep sleep, a much needed rest after discovering the news articles and other assorted notes had been removed from the hiding place. She cleared the cobwebs from her head and followed the voice to Langford's room. He was on his cell phone looking out the window. He turned when he heard her footsteps and motioned for her to sit.

"I'm sorry, Angel, I know you thought highly of Bowman," Langford said into the phone, glancing at Ella.

Ella's eyes widened.

"Okay, I'll see you in a few days." Langford turned off the phone and slid it into his pocket.

"Bad news?" Ella asked.

"Yes, Ella. Bowman Whitmire died this morning. Latisha found him in the bar on the floor."

"Oh, how sad. I'm sure Angel is upset," Ella said, concerned.

"She is, and she's coming back early. Losing Newton and now Bowman." Langford dropped his head in despair.

"I'm sure Bitty already knows. News spreads fast through Sandy Creek. I'll call her and check on her. Bowman was a big part of Sandy Creek, and he did a lot for people in the community, even if he was a bit crooked," said Ella.

She stood and left the room, leaving Langford to his thoughts.

Sadness seemed to engulf the house. All was quiet. Ella's guests were in their rooms with their own thoughts and concerns. She made a cup of tea and stepped out the back door. The sun was on its slide into the depths of the Soul River swamp. She loved this time of the day. Long cast shadows slowly stretched across the yard, always revealing a flower or something new springing to life in its glow.

Ella's heart felt heavy for Bowman's family. She was glad she had taken the time to see Bowman and learn the truth about her young husband, Jacob.

She thought about her brother, Newton, and all he had endured through his life, especially when their father was living. She could no longer carry the load of the secrets of her father and what he had done to her, controlling her life with threats and bullying.

The horrid memories were burning a hole in Ella's heart. Somehow she needed to find a way to release her pain. The great old house loomed over her. She could no longer care for the place. Hiring help for housekeeping went against her principles. She always took care of her own business.

She heard the back door slam and saw Langford walk out and take a seat in the swing. He didn't notice her standing alone by the cornfield. She quietly walked up to him from behind and saw he had the news articles and notes she had been looking for. She cleared her throat.

Langford turned around, surprised to see her.

Ella put a fisted hand on her hip. "I see you're the one who took Daddy's private papers."

"Yes, Ella, we did," Langford sighed.

"We?" she asked angrily.

"Yes. Tobias and I are trying to get to the truth about the man. You're not the only one affected by our father's psychopathic sickness," Langford said impatiently.

Ella flew into a rage. "You have no idea of the pain I've endured my entire life. I have held everything close to the cuff to keep my family name unsoiled."

Tobias stepped out the back door to the commotion between the two. "Hey, calm down, Ella," Tobias pleaded.

Hazel eyes blazing, she pointed a crooked bony finger at Tobias. "And you, a guest in my house, collaborated with him to expose accusations that are not true."

Ella broke down in tears and fell to the ground. Langford and Tobias reached for her and helped her sit up.

"Calm down now, Ella. It's okay. Everything is going to be okay," Langford sat beside her and put a comforting arm around her.

She cried a river, and it seemed forever before she finally calmed down and got herself under control. Langford helped her stand.

"Come on, Ella, let's go up on the porch and sit. How about a drink?" Langford nodded to Tobias to get the bottle and some glasses.

Ella sat in silence looking away from Langford. Tobias returned and handed her a glass of bourbon.

She took a healthy sip. "Why are y'all hell bent on ruining my name?"

Langford looked at Tobias.

Tobias nodded his head. "Okay, Langford, you win. I'm with you on what we discussed this morning."

"Thank you." Langford paused for a minute to gather his thoughts. "Ella, besides knowing that I'm your half brother because your father raped my mother when she was just a teenager, and that he murdered your husband in cold blood, what else do you know about Wilson Timrod?"

Ella looked at Tobias, then back at Langford. Tears welled up in her eyes once again.

"I know more than any one soul could stand," Ella looked away from the two men.

"Can you talk about it, Ella?" Langford asked compassionately "We promise not to say anything to anyone. This will be our secret, but you need to talk to us so we can help you."

"Help me? No one can help me. I'll live the rest of my life with my terrible memories."

"Ella," her newly found brother took her hands in his, "tell us. You need to tell us." Langford gently pushed.

Ella took a healthy drink, wiped away a tear, and looked at Tobias. "On the day Mary Lou Reese disappeared, Newton was home. Daddy must have thought Newton was away with Bitty and me."

She took a deep breath then continued, still looking at Tobias. "From a window upstairs, Newton saw Daddy push the girl into his car. Newton also saw you across the road, out of Daddy's sight, watching. It wasn't until days later that Newton came to me and told me what he had seen, and who else had observed the abduction. Newton insisted we say something to the authorities, but I refused to allow him to speak of what he saw."

She shook her head in disgust. "I knew all of this, but I couldn't go against my father. I was so terribly afraid of him."

Ella cried a little more, then went on. "Newton was devastated. He hated the man intensely and was angry with me, because I kept my mouth shut and made him do the same. That was really when we lost each other."

Tobias was in shock. "Why didn't you come forward?"

Through her tears, Ella looked Tobias in the eye. "Do you think at that time our sheriff, who was so far under my father's control, would believe such a story? And what do you think would've happened to Newton and me? Tobias, if you had come forward, you would most likely be dead now." Ella slammed her glass down on the table.

Tobias leaned back in his chair and looked off into the distance. After a couple of minutes he spoke. "You're right, Ella. That's why my Granddaddy Chainy ran me off and told me not to come back to the barns. He knew what Wilson Timrod was capable of. He knew he killed Mary Lou, and he turned his head to save his skin and mine."

"Of course I'm right. Your granddaddy knew a lot. He kept his mouth shut and his eyes open. He may have played dumb a lot, but he was smart to what my father was up to and didn't want you, his precious grandson, getting in trouble with Wilson Timrod."

They all picked up their glasses and sipped, until Ella was ready to continue.

"A year or so later, Daddy had a stroke and became bedridden. He was still mean as a snake. He treated Newton like a redheaded step-child; talked to him like he was an idiot. But Newton persevered, wanting to bring Daddy to justice.

"One day, Newton came to me and pleaded with me to help him kill Daddy. I couldn't believe what I was hearing. I told him no, absolutely not, and he'd better not attempt it on his own. Newton was still angry with me about Mary Lou's death.

"A few days after our conversation, I went to Daddy's room to check on him. I passed by Newton's room, and I knew by the light under his door that he was home. It was late, around midnight. Daddy was fine. He was sleeping."

Ella sighed deeply. "I don't know if I should say anymore."

She fell silent for a minute. Finally, she spoke. "I stood over Daddy, and I whispered in his ear how I hated him for what he did to me. I told him he was a murderer and a pervert. His eyes opened, and he had a panicked look in them. I quickly turned and left the room."

Langford encouraged her to go on, promising it would stay between the three of them. "Please, Ella, tell us everything. I swear it stays between us."

Ella hung her head. Her voice trembled. "Early the next morning, Newton walked into my bedroom. I was still asleep. He turned on the light. I sat up, stunned. He was holding a pillow. I said, 'Newton, what is going on?"

She stopped, wiped a tear away, took a deep breath and looked up toward the sky. Her voice trembled. "Newton held the pillow up, looked at me, and said, 'I have taken care of our problem.

He's dead.' "

"I jumped up and ran to Daddy's room. There he was, faced contorted, dead as a doornail. I turned, and Newton was standing behind me with the pillow. I took it from him, found a fresh one and put it under Daddy's head. I took the one Newton used to suffocate him and stuffed it as far as I could in the back of my closet, covering it with blankets and shoe boxes. It's still there to this day." She leaned back and covered her face with her hands.

Langford looked completely surprised. "In all of Newton's conversations with me, he never shared this."

"Newton stood staring at my father. It seemed like forever before he spoke to me. He looked at me with the coldest expression, and what he said next completely caught me off guard."

Neither Tobias, nor Langford could breath.

Ella pushed another tear off her cheek. "He said, 'I know Daddy had been raping you, and you should know he came to my room, as well.' "

Ella covered her face in shame and spoke through her hands. "Without another word, Newton turned and left the room. Our estrangement continued until the day he killed himself. We didn't speak of it again. I never really knew my brother after the morning he confessed." Ella crossed her arms over her chest and cried.

Langford stood and walked to the edge of the porch. Leaned on the rail. "So, what did you do next?"

"That morning I called Gaylord Willard and told him my father had died in his sleep. They came out and took him to the funeral home. No one suspected anything. Everyone in Riverton knew he was sick."

Tobias and Langford looked at each other in disbelief.

"That's it. The bastard was dead, and my life changed forever. Newton's did, too, but the years had driven a stake between him and me. As I said, he never brought it up, nor did I, especially after learning Newton was a victim as well. I really think he wanted to kill Daddy to get the satisfaction of watching him die."

Ella stood up and walked to the door, looking back at Langford and Tobias. "My father sexually abused me for years. I will never get over it. It sticks to me like tar and feathers. I suffer everyday in my life. Sometimes I can bury the pain and not have flashbacks of him climbing into my bed late in the night. He would wear that black cloth mask, but I knew it was him. I shudder to think what my poor brother went through."

She disappeared into the house.

The two men sat silently stunned, pondering what to do. It was all so surreal, but considering all the abuse Ella and Newton endured, it was justice.

Langford spoke first. "Newton told me this was going on with Ella, but he never said it happened to him."

Langford sat quietly for a few minutes, drinking the last sips of bourbon in his glass.

Tobias stood up. "I guess my heartbreak and misery is nothing compared to what those two went through. What should we do?" Tobias asked.

"Right now, Ella needs our support. I'm afraid she may go down the same road as Newton if we don't get her some help. I'm going to see where she went and talk with her about seeing a doctor," Langford said with concern.

Ella wanted to sit on the front porch in silence. She fixed herself another bourbon and went to the front of the house, away from the two men. She was numb from her confession and felt the need to close her eyes and sleep. Once again, she remembered the bottle of valium in her side table. Could that be her answer?

She heard the door open and saw Langford. "What do you want?"

"Ella, please listen to what I have to say. As a physician, I can see you are hurting inside. I see this a lot in my practice. As your half brother, would you consider coming to Charleston and living with me? There, we could find a good therapist to help you through this."

Ella laughed sarcastically. "I'm not stupid, Langford. As soon as I disclose that my brother murdered my father, it will have to be reported. No, I'll not discuss it again. The two of you know the truth now, and I hope I can depend on your word not to tell a soul."

Langford wouldn't give up. "Are you going to stay here alone and live out the rest of your life swallowed up by the horrible memories this house represents?"

Ella turned away and shook her hand to shoo him off. "Please leave me alone. I've had enough today. Let me enjoy my drink and slip into my fantasy world where I find comfort."

He could tell the bourbon had gone to her

head. She was slurring her words a bit.

Langford stepped in front of her. "Drinking this away isn't the answer."

Ella smiled. "No, it's not, but I've been doing it for years, and it seems to help. Sometimes."

Langford's face grew stern. "I know you've been toying with suicide."

Ella stood up. "I'm going to my room, and what you just said is ridiculous."

Later in the evening, Langford and Tobias went for a walk. They were trying to decide how to handle her confession.

Tobias had a suggestion. "Langford, let's talk to Billy Miles tomorrow and see what he has to say. We won't use Ella's name, but we could present a hypothetical scenario to get his feedback."

"Tobias, Captain Miles will put it together. He'll know just what we're talking about."

Tobias smiled. "That's right. He will, and he'll answer without asking."

"I'll let you try, since you were school chums, and, of course, you have the gift of a seasoned courtroom attorney," suggested Langford.

"Okay, I'll do it when we meet him for a beer

tomorrow," agreed Tobias.

The following morning, Ella appeared in the kitchen. She seemed a little better and engaged the two in conversation about the weather. Langford found this a bit odd. Their last words were not friendly, and he was pretty sure she was headed for a major breakdown. She rambled on about the garden, and then, out of the blue, she knocked them for a loop.

"Langford, Tobias, as soon as I get Newton's ashes, I'm driving straight to the bridge and scattering them. You are welcome to join me there. After that, I'd like you both to leave my house."

The two were taken aback by her abruptness.

"Okay, we'll vacate the premises, as you wish," Langford said, looking for Tobias's reaction.

"Thank you. Now, I must call the funeral home and see when Newton will be ready."

Ella turned to leave the room. "One other thing; could you two bring down the boxes of books and leave them on the porch? The library is coming over this morning to pick them up.

"Of course, we'll take care of that. What about the artwork?" asked Tobias.

"Take it down and drop it off at my attorney's

office, it's only five pieces." She left the room.

They could hear her steps fading into the bowels of the house.

"Well, I guess she's tired of company," Tobias joked.

Langford looked grim. "This is no joking matter. I don't like what I'm seeing and hearing from Ella."

It wasn't long before Ella returned. "I have good news. Newton's ashes are ready, and I'm on my way to pick them up. I'll stop at the bridge and scatter them. If you're joining me, maybe you should pack your things before we leave."

A van from the library pulled up in the drive.

"Oh good, the men from the library are here. Langford please take care of it, if you don't mind. I'll meet you at the bridge in about an hour. Don't be late." She walked out with purse in hand.

Two young men stood at the back door. Langford was relieved he and Tobias didn't have to tote the boxes down stairs. *Leave it to youth.*

"Right this way." Langford showed them to Newton's room where they easily lifted and ran up and down the stairs with the books. Langford signed a receipt and they were gone.

"Well, could you give me a lift to a hotel?" Langford asked Tobias.

Tobias shook his head. "We'll go to my folks' place. It's furnished. We can drop off the paintings after she scatters Newton's ashes. Maybe not what we're both used to, but it will suffice for a day or so, at least until after Bowman's funeral."

Ella waited in Gaylord's office while he retrieved the ashes.

Ella stood stiffly, dressed in black for the occasion. Gaylord came in carrying the box with Newton's ashes, sat it on the table and asked Ella to sign a few forms.

"Okay, Ella, he's all yours. Shall I send the bill or would you —"

"How much do I owe?" Ella interrupted. She whipped out her checkbook.

Gaylord started itemizing the bill.

"The box we put him in for the cremation . . ."

"Just give me the total, Gaylord. I don't care about all your extras," she said rudely.

Gaylord was caught off guard. Ella had never spoken to him in such a tone. "$3200.00," he replied.

Ella quickly wrote out the check. "Here you are.

Thank you for all you have done for me and my family over the years. You're a good man." She turned and walked out, leaving him speechless.

The dark water of the Soul River slowly swirled around the pylons, leaving tiny little vortexes as it passed under the bridge, making its way to the sea. Dragonflies fluttered in the air, touching down to the water in sporadic movement. Downriver, a bullfrog croaked. The day was warming up. Swarming balls of gnats floated in the air. The mud turtles quickly abandoned the rotting log they were sunning on when the sound of voices echoed down the river. Black as tar with no bottom in sight, the Soul looked mysterious and foreboding.

Tobias leaned against the concrete railings of the Wilson Timrod Bridge looking into the depths of the Soul River. Langford looked down the road toward Riverton. His mind somewhere else. He was worried about Ella; he felt like she was getting ready to do something horrible.

"You know Langford, my dad and I would come down here to fish. There was a little path we took down to the river and got underneath the bridge. We had our cane poles, a can of night crawlers. We'd sit for hours watching our corks bob in the black water. He and I had some wonderful conversations about life and other interesting topics. We'd take our catch of bream and catfish home. Daddy would clean them up. Mama would cook a big old pot of grits and tomatoes. My mom would make him fry the fish outside. She didn't like the smell in the house. Those were really special times. I had angels looking out after me, my dad and my grandad."

"Langford ceased his preoccupation with wondering where Ella might be, and walked over to where Tobias stood. "You know Tobias it doesn't matter about material possessions. As long as you have a loving family and home, that's all that matters."

Tobias laughed. "You're right Langford. Look at poor Ella and Newton. All the land and huge house but their childhoods were miserable. All I ever knew was love and family."

The sound of a car approaching made them look up. It was Ella. She pulled over. Langford opened her door. With not a word said, Ella walked to the railing of the bridge. Opening the box, she pulled out the plastic bag that held Newton's ashes.

She turned to Langford. "Do you want to say any words before I do this?"

"I was hoping you would, Ella," Langford said.

She untied the plastic bag. "Newton, I am truly

sorry for you and for how we suffered so much. I 've always loved you, Brother, no matter our differences."

That said, Ella turned the bag upside down. The gray ashes drifted through the air then fell into the water. They formed an abstract swirl on the surface and slowly floated down the Soul to parts unknown.

Langford watched as Newton's ashes continued swirling down the river. Some caught up in the edges of the weeds, but for the most part, Newton was gone. All Langford had now were the memories of the times they spent together laughing and enjoying a drink on the porch at Langford's Charleston home. He braced his hands against the bridge rail, dropped his head and wept.

Tobias stepped next to Langford, wrapped his arm around his shoulder and gave him a hug. Ella stood back watching, waiting for Langford to gather himself before she said her goodbye.

Finally, she interrupted the two men. "Langford, I'm leaving. I want to thank you for all you've done for me."

She turned her head away, looking down at the ground. "Especially allowing me to tell my side and the truth."

She turned to Tobias. "Tobias, I'm sorry about your dear friend, Mary Lou Reese. I can't fix what my father did. I don't believe anyone can. I am extremely proud of you for all you've accomplished. I'm going home now."

Ella turned away abruptly and walked to her car.

Langford followed her. "Ella, we're still brother and sister, and I'm always here for you."

She said nothing more, got in her car and drove away. The two men watched her car disappear down the road.

22

The Fire

W ell, Tobias, where does this leave us? Do we talk with Billy Miles as we planned?" Langford asked.

Tobias rubbed his forehead with frustration. "God, this place. I can't wait to get the hell out of here. No, we don't, Langford. We'll meet him as planned, but I think we should just drop it. She's right. I can't fix it. And neither can Ella Timrod. She's as messed up as the rest of her family. Except for you," Tobias added with a smile.

Langford looked at his watch. "It's noon. Let's drive into Riverton and have lunch."

Tobias agreed. "Also, afterward, we'll do a little looking around until it's time to meet Billy."

Tobias headed to the car, but Langford hung back, looking down the road toward Ella's home. *What is she up to? She's not acting right.*

Sam's Burger Barn was located at the end of Main Street in Riverton, across from the abandoned tobacco warehouses. Weeds grew around the edges of the old warehouses. A few vehicles were parked in front of the restaurant.

Tobias pulled up near the front door. He found a notepad and wrote while speaking to Langford. "I will have a cheeseburger, Carolina style, with fries and a Coke. What do you want?"

"We're not going in?" Langford questioned.

"Nope. I don't want my clothes to smell like fried food. I got that from my mom."

"I see. I trust you won't let me do something I might regret. I'll have the same."

Tobias grinned. "You sure? It's a lot of food."

Langford thought for a moment. "What's on the burger?"

"Oh, chili and onions, with mustard."

Langford laughed. "Do they have any food that won't kill you?"

"Not really. Come on, Langford, go for it, just this once," Tobias urged.

"Well, okay," Langford grimaced.

A young boy stood at the front door. Tobias motioned for him to come over to the car.

"Yes, sir, what can I get you?" The boy smiled.

Tobias gave him their order and handed him the note and money. "Tell Sam we'll be out back."

"Will do," the boy replied, tipping his ball cap.

"Keep the change," said Tobias.

"Thank you, sir," His smile grew huge.

Tobias drove back to the gravel parking lot, got out of the car, stretched, and looked around.

Langford was confused as to why they were going to sit out back. "So why out here?" he asked.

"Memories, my friend, memories."

Tobias threw his legs over the wooden seat and nestled up to the picnic style table. It was worn and slick on the edges with a few names carved in the wood. Tobias searched the table until he found his name and a date.

"This table has been around a long time. It was brand new when I carved my name in it, way back in my high school years, but it isn't the table that brings back a deep and moving memory. I'll always remember having an impressionable conversation with my Daddy one day at this place; way before this table was even here."

His thoughts wandered to his childhood. "Daddy worked at the tobacco sales. It was one of his many side jobs so he could make enough to take care of a wife and three kids. A few times, he would let me come into Riverton with him. I was just a little fellow. So, he would pull up in front of this place at lunch, and a boy would come over to take his order. We'd drive back and pick up our order at the back door. Then we'd sit right here with the rest of the black folks and eat."

"I see, Tobias." Langford knew right where he was going with this story.

Tobias looked off toward town. "I asked Daddy why we ate out behind the restaurant. I'll never forget what he said. The sadness and gravity in his voice as he explained the way of those times resonated with me.

"Times have changed. Black and white folks enjoy each other's company, but It's still a biased world we live in, with people who are racist. That's their problem, not mine. Look at us. We've become good friends over a short period. We look beyond our skin color and respect each other's minds. We see more important issues besides black and white."

The restaurant's back door flew open, and a young man came out. "So, you sitting at the segregation table, Tobias?"

The young black man put the tray down. Filled with so much food, Langford could hear his arteries clogging.

Tobias stood. They did their handshake thing and hugged. "Sam, this is my good friend, Langford Wallace, from Charleston."

Langford stood and shook Sam's hand.

"Sam, here, is my brother's son. With a little help from Uncle Tobias, Sam and I bought this place a few years back. I sort of had a soft spot for it, if you know what I mean." Tobias laughed.

"Yes, I understand now." Langford nodded.

"Tobias, I have to get back to work. I'm talking with Jay Sumpter about a partnership. We've got a new idea for Riverton," Sam said.

"Yeah, what sort of idea?" Tobias was curious.

"Oh, Uncle, it's good. Jay's going to grow organic vegetables, and we're going to open an upscale diner that serves healthy food and not this greasy stuff," Sam said, pointing to the burgers.

Langford looked at his food and moaned.

Tobias smiled at Sam. "Sounds great, Sam, but you know these folks around Riverton are going to scoff at healthy food."

"At some point, we have to make changes in this town, or it will die," Sam said confidently.

"If you need anything, let me know," Tobias hugged Sam.

Langford watched the young man walk away. "Nice kid. He's your brother's son?"

"Yep." Tobias took a bite of his burger. Mustard dripped from the corner of his mouth.

"Sam can grill a good burger." He smiled and wiped his mouth.

Langford was still trying to decide on how to bite into his burger without spilling chili and mustard all over the place.

"Just do it, Langford. Eat up." Tobias smiled.

Langford finally managed a bite and moaned with satisfaction. "Oh, this is wonderful." He took another bite, put down the sloppy burger, and wiped his mouth. "So, where is your brother?"

"Dead." Tobias continued to eat.

"What happened to him, if you don't mind me asking?"

"He drowned in the river." Tobias looked away.

"I'm sorry, Tobias."

"It was an unfortunate accident. Drunks and fishing boats can be hazardous when put together." Tobias sighed and shook his head.

Langford had enough of his Carolina burger and knew he would have to pay penance for eating it. He covered it with his napkin. "Done, Tobias. I cannot eat another bite."

By 4:00 p.m., they had located the River Room on the backstreet of Riverton. Langford was amazed at the old, closed, and shuttered buildings around town. It was a shame to see it wasting away.

Inside, at the bar of the River Room, Billy Miles had a table for them and already had his beer. "What are y'all drinking?"

Billy stood and waited for the two to decide.

Langford saw the selection wasn't so great, so he ordered a Bud Lite. Tobias went with the Old Milwaukee.

"Candy, how about an Old Milwaukee and a Bud Lite?" Billy shouted to the barmaid.

"On your tab, Billy?" she plopped two beers on the bar.

"Yep, got this round." Billy slid down into his chair and handed Tobias and Langford their beers.

Tobias took a sip. "At least it's ice cold."

Langford laughed, then took a swig. "Oh, boy, nice and cold."

Billy looked at the two and couldn't help likening them to a couple of strange-looking fellows who had wandered off the interstate into town.

"I hope some of these boys here don't suspect you two are sweet on each other," he said, laughing at his funny comment.

Tobias grabbed Billy by the neck. "Now, Billy Miles, you know you're my main man."

The two laughed until they cried.

Langford looked lost while Tobias and Billy told old stories, yet he enjoyed hearing them laugh and reminisce.

At about beer number three, Langford asked Billy if he had any dirt on Tobias.

Tobias stood up to go to the men's room. "When I get back, we'll talk dirt."

"So, Langford, how do you like our little piece of heaven?" Billy asked, finishing his beer.

"It's a nice town. I had a heart-stopping burger, visited a beautiful swimming hole, and spent almost two weeks with Ella Timrod." Langford didn't want to talk too much more about Ella.

Billy leaned back in his chair while peeling the label off his beer bottle. "I guess Tobias told you how we became friends years ago."

Langford nodded.

"Did he tell you about Mary Lou Reese?" Billy sipped his beer.

"Yeah, he told me all about her; her unpleasant death." Langford was surprised Billy brought up Mary Lou Reese. Tobias still hadn't returned from the men's room. He watched Billy's face change to serious.

Billy leaned close to Langford. The beer had loosened his tongue a little. "I remember how heart-broken Tobias was. We were in high school together. It was our senior year, and I'm here to tell you that Mary Lou's death killed him. Did Tobias tell you about them swimming together and all?"

Billy drank more beer and kept talking.

"I was going through some old files, doing a little cleaning back in the evidence room one day, and came across the murder report. Of course, I had to sit down and read it."

Caught off guard, Langford grew uncomfortable with their conversation.

"What did Tobias tell you about the day Mary Lou disappeared?" Billy asked.

"I know what Tobias saw, and that's enough."

Billy emptied his beer. "I'm guessing, Dr. Wallace, you know more than you like." Billy winked at Langford.

Tobias returned with another round, much to Langford's relief.

Before Billy could say anything more, his cell phone rang. "Hello. What?" Billy asked, looking startled.

Billy looked at Langford and Tobias. "Y'all, we got a five-alarm fire at the Timrod house. They're calling trucks from the next county over. I gotta go. I'm a volunteer fireman. You can follow me if you want. Just stay up with me."

Langford looked anxiously at Tobias. "Well?"

"I'm good, Langford. Let's go."

Billy's pickup sped out of the parking lot and down the road, with Tobias and Langford in hot pursuit.

In the distance, they could see smoke and flames.

"Oh, my God, I hope Ella isn't in the house," said Langford.

Billy pulled up behind other trucks, and Tobias pulled in behind him. Firefighters ran around with hoses, and water trucks made runs from the Soul River to the house. It was a crazy, chaotic scene.

As Billy was pulling on his gear, Tobias and Langford ran to see if they could locate Ella. They couldn't find her anywhere and started asking around.

A young fireman approached the two men. "Are you Dr. Wallace?"

"Yes, I am. Where is Ella Timrod?" Langford asked in a panic.

The young fireman pointed to the garage. "She asked for you, Dr. Wallace. She won't leave. She refuses to get out of the old car. She has an empty bottle of pills, and a gun she pointed at us, so we can't take her by force. We need to get her out. We're concerned the garage might spark."

Langford looked off toward the garage. He could see Ella sitting in the driver's seat, holding onto the steering wheel. A county deputy and a fireman, ready with a water hose, stood before the car.

"Come on, Tobias, help me," said Langford.

The two maneuvered around hoses and fire-fighters until they got close enough to Ella. He looked at her through the windshield.

"Ella, honey, please get out of the car. Please, let me help you."

Ella continued her empty stare. By the look in her eyes, Langford knew she had checked out. The Valium was taking effect. He opened the door and slowly knelt next to her. The bottle of valium was empty, and the gun was now in her lap.

In a slow and soft tone, Langford asked Ella if he could have the gun. With no response from her, he carefully lifted it and removed it from her lap.

Ella turned and looked at him sadly. "Langford, I have finally cleared my conscience. No more shame. Hopefully, I can rest now."

She collapsed onto the steering wheel.

Langford and Tobias held her and carried her to a waiting ambulance with the help of a couple of firefighters. Langford climbed into the front seat of the ambulance while the paramedic immediately started working on Ella. Her heart rate slowed, and Langford begged them to hurry to the hospital. Tobias followed in his car.

The small Riverton medical facility wasn't prepared to meet Ella's needs. Langford asked if she could be transported to Charleston. She was airlifted to the Medical University Hospital. The following day she woke up in the psychiatric ward.

A few days later, traces of smoke still drifted from the fire. It took many days to put out all the hot spots. The house was gone, and the garage with the Cadillac eventually burned down, too. The only structures left were the old tobacco barns across the road.

All over Riverton, gossip-filled the beauty shops and Johnny's Barber Shop. Ella Timrod had gone crazy and burned her home to the ground.

23

Charleston

Ella sat in her therapist's office, Dr. Addison Covington. Langford knew him well. He considered him one of the best psychologists in Charleston. Covington waited patiently for Ella to speak. She drank some water and looked over at him, dreading the moment but knowing the truth needed unpacking.

She began her tale of horror and abuse living under the power of her psychopathic father. "My father started coming to my bed when I was five years old. By the time I was ten, I knew enough to expect his late-night visits. Sometimes, he would be away on business, and if he returned late at night, he would always come to my room. I could hear his footsteps approaching from down the hall, and then my door would open and shut. He always wore that black cloth mask, but I knew it was my father. The mask, though, was terrifying. I was so young, just a kid."

She took a deep breath. "When my mother died giving birth to my brother, Newton, I knew I didn't have a chance. I knew things would get far worse for me." Ella choked back tears.

"Daddy hired a maid to take care of baby Newton. The maid and Newton lived together in one of the downstairs guest rooms, and she cared for Newton until he was five or six."

Ella paused and seemed to drift away.

"Ella, you have to talk to me so I can help you," said Dr. Covington softly.

She came back to herself and continued. "I left my body each time he appeared at my bedside. He always wore that damned black mask. It frightened me to the point that I would go away in my mind; so far away that I didn't even feel the pain when he assaulted me."

"It's called a dissociative disorder, and it happens to people who have suffered great trauma, especially in their childhood," said Dr. Covington.

"Whatever you call it, it helped me not feel so terrified. I was able to get through the assaults."

"What about your older sister, Mary Kay? Did your father assault her?" he asked.

Ella shook her head and shrugged her shoulders. "I don't know, but I assume he did. Mary Kay was always a bit sickly. I never knew why and often wondered if it was something he did to her."

Ella was silent for a few minutes. Dr. Covington waited for her to continue when she was ready.

"Some nights, I would hear his car pull up to the garage. I'd climb out of bed, go to the window and watch him walk through the dark toward the house. I would run to my bed and curl up in a tight ball, hoping he would pass by my door and leave me be."

"Go on, Ella," he encouraged.

She looked over at Dr. Covington. "I can't do it anymore today. Can we stop for now?"

Dr. Covington looked at the time. "Sure, Ella, our time is almost up. You did wonderfully today. Now, remember to be good to yourself for the rest of the day. Get some rest."

Ella looked at him. "You can't imagine my fear, knowing he was on his way to my room."

Dr. Covington looked at her and then made a note. "Ella, I would like to discuss your fear at our next meeting. I'm giving you an assignment. Write about your fear and bring it to our next session."

She nodded. "I can do that." Ella stood up, thanked him, and left the office.

Langford sat on a bench reading his book. Ella exited Dr. Covington's office. He could tell it had been a rough hour by how she carried herself. They walked together in silence, and the drive home wasn't any different. Ella stared out the window, lost in another time and place.

Visits with Dr. Covington always left her exhausted, and all she wanted to do was lie down and rest. Langford knew she was tired. He helped Ella into the car and headed straight for home, where she retreated to her room.

Thursday morning, Langford's phone rang. It was Tobias Williams.

"Langford, how are you, my good friend?" Tobias asked excitedly. "And how is Ella doing?"

"Oh, Ella's making some progress. She has good and bad days, but I think she'll pull through. Has it been almost a year, Tobias, since we last spoke?"

"It has, and I feel bad I haven't called more often. Since getting back to Boston, I've had a full plate of cases."

Tobias went straight to his reason for the call. "You know the extra hundred acres of land Ella sold to Jay Sumpter?"

"Well, of course," Langford replied. "I played a role in her selling all her land except for the house site. I'm glad Jay was able to afford more land."

"Langford, guess what Jay Sumpter dug up while plowing down near the river swamp on his new parcel of land?"

Langford fell silent for a few seconds. "Don't tell me . . ."

"Bodies, dead bodies, Langford. Confirmed to be the skeletal remains of nineteen women, mostly young girls."

"Tobias, this will kill Ella. I'm not sure I want her to know."

"Langford, I was right all along. I'm driving to Riverton now. I should be there late tonight. Please come up and join me."

Langford thought for a moment. "If I can get Angel to stay with Ella for a day, I will join you. I'll let you know."

Langford hung up the phone, thought for a moment, and called Angel. He gave her the news. She was more than willing to help out.

Later in the day, Ella was up and walking around the yard. Langford approached her with two glasses of bourbon. "Hey, Ella, how's my sis doing this afternoon?"

"I'm good. I feel like my therapy is going well, and I like Dr. Covington." She forced a slight smile.

They sat in the wicker chairs facing the inlet. Langford took a sip and turned to her. "Ella, I need to go to Riverton and meet with Tobias for a couple of days. Do you mind if Angel comes over and stays with you until I get back?"

Ella could tell he was up to something. He wasn't a good liar. "Can I come with you? I'd like to see Bitty. I haven't seen my friend in a long time."

"But, Ella, you told me you never wanted to go back there. What is this change of mind?"

"I'm feeling better. I want to go back and see just what I did to my house." She sipped her drink and watched his eyes.

Langford thought about what Ella said and just how much he should tell her. "Okay, here's the truth. I don't believe in holding back information that might help you with your past."

Ella perked up. "I'm waiting."

"Ella, you know the extra hundred acres you sold to Jay Sumpter?"

She nodded.

"Jay was plowing near the swamp and uncovered many skeletal remains. It turns out they were the remains of young girls."

Langford paused and waited for a response from Ella. He could tell the memory gears were working in her head. She seemed to be far away, and what he had just told her didn't appear to register with her.

Then she smiled. "I just love the smell of the sea and watching the tide roll in and out. That's something I've never really experienced before. There's nothing dark and gloomy here like it was on the farm."

She looked at him straight on. "That's good news, Langford. Deep down inside, I always knew my father was a killer. He was an evil man, and I'm sure he killed those girls and buried them on the farm, but can anyone prove he did it? I will do whatever it takes to find the truth."

Langford wrung his hands. He spoke his next words carefully. "Ella, we don't have proof, but I guess he did it."

She looked at him and smiled again. "I'm going with you, Langford. Bitty told me there's a new hotel out on the interstate. We can stay there. I'll pack my bag."

Langford called Angel to let her know she didn't need to come over and stay with Ella. Angel decided she would go with them, as well. It would be an excellent time to see her mother and father.

The burnt-out ruins of the Timrod house still stood. Police tape surrounded the place. All that remained were budding flowers that had somehow survived the trampling of fire hoses and men in heavy boots, not to mention the extreme heat of the fire.

It was hard for Ella to look at the ruins. She didn't remember much about that day except sitting in her father's car, waiting to die. According to the fire chief, she had taken gasoline and poured it into the main hall. That was the hotspot or the beginning of the fire. It engulfed the house rapidly, and it was too late by the time the first truck arrived. They could only try to keep some control over the billowing flames, which seemed to reach hundreds of feet in the air.

Langford and Ella slowly walked around the yard. She had come a long way over the last year, having spent months in a private hospital after a few weeks in the psychiatric ward at the Medical University Hospital. Despite her age, Ella's grit and stamina had carried her through.

"Langford, I can't believe I burned my house."

"Ella, honey, you had a good reason to destroy something that reminded you of your traumatic past."

They returned to the small group of people waiting for Ella to sign the release to have her father exhumed. Bitty sat in Langford's car while Angel and Tobias stood talking to the sheriff. A couple of agents from the state forensic lab waited by their van. They had spent the last four days digging up remains and compiling evidence.

Tobias stared across the road at the old barns. He reflected on his boyhood days working with his grandfather, whose job it had been to keep an eye on Mr. Timrod's empire. Tobias recalled seeing his grandfather fiddling around the barns, cleaning up, all hunched over from years of walking under the tobacco hanging inside. What did his grandfather know?

Ella still owned the ten acres the burnt shell of her house stood on. She had sold all the other land, but not a soul was interested in the house site. She and Langford strolled over to where the agents and Sheriff Chastine were waiting.

"Ms. Timrod, are you ready to go to the cemetery and get this over with?" the sheriff asked her.

"Yes, Sheriff, I am."

Ella smiled at him. Her face appeared relaxed and soft. The stressful look typically on her face had vanished.

Sheriff Chastine gave Langford the papers needed to sign to have Wilson Timrod's remains exhumed for DNA testing. Langford opened each page for Ella, and she signed her name.

"There you are, Sheriff." She handed him his pen and turned to Langford.

"Shall we go, brother, and watch the excitement?"

In Riverton, at the cemetery, a team of men stood by for the go-ahead to start digging. Gaylord Willard gave the backhoe operator the word to begin. A van waited to take the casket to the forensic lab in Columbia.

At another cemetery, state police exhumed the remains of Mary Lou Reese.

Tobias couldn't believe it was finally happening. The truth about the many victims would come out, and Mary Lou's killer would be exposed.

From the back seat of Langford's car, Ella and Bitty anxiously watched as the casket was lifted out and placed in a van.

"Bitty, except for my late husband, you have been the only person in my life who has given me happiness. Thank you for all you've done for me over the many years."

Bitty squeezed Ella's hand. "Ella, I have always been your friend, and if you need me, you just call me. You can tell me anything. I'm here for you."

Langford opened the car door. "Ella, Sheriff Chastine said we could go. They'll most likely be here for a few more days, wrapping up, making sure they've found all the remains. How about we head to Charleston?"

Ella agreed. She had become accustomed to consenting lately. She seemed to feel better and more comfortable with others helping her make decisions.

She hugged Bitty and Tobias and said her goodbyes. Angel decided to visit with her mother for the weekend. Tobias was going to his nephew's house.

Gossip was all over Riverton and became the talk of the state for years. Because so many nosy people drove down the road to see where the serial killer had lived, they paved County Road 316.

Ella finally sold the house site, and the new owners sold all the old machines, removed the junk, and took down the barns. The ground the barns had stood on was graded and seeded with wildflowers. Across the road, a young couple built a beautiful new home. Ella's flowers still held their ground and appeared every spring.

Ella thought her best move was her petition to the state to rename the Wilson Timrod Bridge to the Newton Thomas Timrod Memorial Bridge.

She continued to get well, but deep inside, the memories of her abuse still haunted her.

She enjoyed living with her brother. Langford afforded Ella the life Newton had always wanted for her. She started coming out of her shell and found a friend or two, but Bitty remained her oldest and best friend, and they visited each other regularly.

A few more years passed. It was spring, and Ella was enjoying her after-dinner glass of bourbon. Langford and Angel were in the kitchen sipping wine and laughing as they cleaned up the dinner dishes. Langford had retired and was missing a lot of the medical world. The two were engrossed in conversation about a new medical procedure Angel had recently learned.

Ella sat in the wicker chair, sipped her bourbon, and enjoyed the late-day show of color. The setting sun exposed the pluff mud with its gray and lavender hues against a sea of yellow-green marsh grass. In the west, the sun slowly slid behind a faraway line of pines. It reflected off the inlet, giving beautiful color to the entire area. The azaleas and dogwoods, Ella's favorites, were in bloom. A cool breeze flowed across her face, making her feel refreshed and new again. The smell of the salt marsh mingled in the air. Ella looked out at the beauty before her and smiled. Her hand fell limp, and she slumped in her chair. Her glass dropped to the wooden deck and shattered.

Ella's soul stepped out of her old body. She saw herself dead. She looked down at the shattered glass. "Langford will never be able to replace this Waterford crystal."

Newton appeared beside her and took her hand. They walked down the steps toward the marsh, fading into the evening dusk.

The End

Dedication

On the morning of April 10th, 2018, George, the love of my life, passed away unexpectedly. When George died, my creative Spirit also died. I didn't want to write, paint, or draw. I was depressed. All I wanted to do was lay on the couch curled up like a cat and sleep. I hid my depression from family and friends pretty well. Deep down inside, I was lost and hurting. Finally, I knew if I didn't put my feet on the floor and do something, I would fall deeper into darkness. So, every day I made myself get up and move. I went to work writing. After four years of fighting through depressive times and forcing myself to work, I finally completed, *Finding the Pieces*, my second novel. Now that it's complete, I will begin a new project. George would expect me to carry on with my writing and other artistic endeavors. He is always in my heart and mind.

This book is in memory of my late husband, the love of my life, George Glass. I love you and miss you.

Acknowledgements

A few people have come into my writing life who have guided and supported me.

Jane Berry, for her continuing friendship and support.

My sister Annelle, for loving me and helping me through my creative journeys and her illustration (Old Tobacco Barn).

Beverly Bruemmer, my head cheerleader. Also, for getting me to the right people. She can light a fire under you.

Amber Pickle for designing and layout. Thank you, Amber, for being so patient.

Dr. Bob Hill, thank you for listening.

About the Author

S ally Glass was born in Conway, South Carolina spending most of her life in the Horry County area. She is a self-taught artist and writer. Sally published her first book in 2005. Before writing *Caleb's Curse,* she directed her talent toward the visual arts.

In late 1990 she and her husband George relocated to the small community of Piney Creek, North Carolina, where she continued her art and writing. In 2018, she lost George, the love of her life.

In the spring of 2020, Sally relocated to Georgia near family.

This novel is her first attempt at reigniting her writing craft after losing her husband.

This story is a sample of the imagination and creativity she has always possessed.

www.ingramcontent.com/pod-product-compliance
Lightning Source LLC
Chambersburg PA
CBHW070850260626
47170CB00007B/2567